ABOUT THE AUTHOR

Barbara Cartland, the world's most famous romantic novelist, who is also an historian, playwright, lecturer, political speaker and television personality, has now written over 623 books and sold over 600 million copies all over the world.

She has also had many historical works published and has written four autobiographies as well as the biographies of her mother and that of her brother, Ronald Cartland, who was the first Member of Parliament to be killed in the last war. This book has a preface by Sir Winston Churchill and has just been published with an introduction by the late Sir Arthur Bryant.

"Love at the Helm" a novel written with the help and inspiration of the late Earl Mountbatten of Burma, Great Uncle of His Royal Highness The Prince of Wales, is being sold for the Mountbatten Memorial Trust.

She has broken the world record for the last seventeen years by writing an average of twenty-three books a year. In the Guinness Book of Records she is listed as the world's top-selling author.

In 1978 she sang an Album of Love Songs with the Royal Philharmonic Orchestra.

In private life Barbara Cartland, who is a Dame of Grace of the Order of St. John of Jerusalem, Chairman of the St. John Council in Hertfordshire and Deputy President of the St. John Ambulance Brigade, has fought for better conditions and salaries for Midwives and Nurses.

She championed the cause for the Elderly in 1956 invoking a Government Enquiry into the "Housing Conditions of Old People".

In 1962 she had the Law of England changed so that Local Authorities had to provide camps for their own Gypsies. This has meant that since then thousands and thousands of Gypsy children have been able to go to School which they had never been able to do in the past, as their caravans were moved every twenty-four hours by the Police.

There are now fourteen camps in Hertfordshire and Barbara Cartland has her own Romany Gypsy Camp called Barbaraville by the Gypsies.

Her designs "Decorating with Love" are being sold all over the U.S.A. and the National Home Fashions League made her in 1981, "Woman of Achievement".

Barbara Cartland's book "Getting Older, Growing Younger" has been published in Great Britain and the U.S.A. and her fifth Cookery Book, "The Romance of Food" is now being used by the House of Commons.

In 1984 she received at Kennedy Airport, America's Bishop Wright Air Industry Award for her contribution to the development of aviation. In 1931 she and two R.A.F. Officers thought of, and carried the first aeroplane-towed glider air-mail.

During the War she was Chief Lady Welfare Officer in Bedfordshire looking after 20,000 Service men and women. She thought of having a pool of Wedding Dresses at the War Office so a Service Bride could hire a gown for the day.

She bought 1,000 secondhand gowns without coupons for the A.T.S., the W.A.A.F.s and the W.R.E.N.S. In 1945 Barbara Cartland received the Certificate of Merit from Eastern Command.

In 1964 Barbara Cartland founded the National Association for Health of which she is the President, as a front for all the Health Stores and for any product made as alternative medicine.

This has now a £500,000,000 turnover a year, with one third going in export.

In January 1988 she received "La Medaille de Vermeil de la Ville de Paris", (The Gold Medal of Paris). This is the highest award to be given by the City of Paris for ACHIEVEMENT – 25 million books sold in France.

In March 1988 Barbara Cartland was asked by the Indian Government to open their Health Resort outside Delhi. This is almost the largest Health Resort in the world.

Barbara Cartland was received with great enthusiasm by her fans, who also fêted her at a Reception in the City and she received the gift of an embossed plate from the Government.

Barbara Cartland was made a Dame of the Order of the British Empire in the 1991 New Year's Honours List, by Her Majesty The Queen for her contribution to literature and for her work for the Community.

AWARDS

1945   Received Certificate of Merit, Eastern Command.

1953   Made a Commander of the Order of St John of Jerusalem. Invested by H.R.H. The Duke of Gloucester at Buckingham Palace.

1972   Invested as Dame of Grace of the Order of St John in London by The Lord Prior, Lord Cacia.

1981   Receives "Achiever of the Year" from the National Home Furnishing Association in Colorado Springs, U.S.A.

1984   Receives Bishop Wright Air Industry Award at Kennedy Airport, for inventing the aeroplane-towed Glider.

1988   Receives from Monsieur Chirac, The Prime Minister, the Gold Medal of the City of Paris, at the Hôtel de la Ville, Paris, for selling 25 million books and giving a lot of employment.

1991   Invested as Dame of the Order of The British Empire, by H.M. The Queen at Buckingham Palace, for her contribution to literature.

The Dare-Devil Duke

Kasia's father, a wealthy Shipping Magnate tells her he has arranged for her to marry Lord Stefelton to save her from fortune-hunters.

Kasia is horrified and says she will only marry for love.

Her father tells her angrily that without him she could not keep herself, and would not know how to earn a penny piece.

Determined to prove him wrong, she takes a job as Governess to a seven-year-old orphan called Simon. He is the nephew of the Duke of Dreghorne and lives at his Castle.

The Duke is a war hero and has the reputation of a dare-devil.

Simon is a difficult child and behaving in an unruly manner so that none of the Duke's relations want him.

Kasia wins his confidence and he begins learning without realising he is doing so.

Then one day out riding Simon and Kasia are kidnapped.

How Kasia solves Simon's problems, and how she loses her heart, is all told in this enchanting and fascinating book, the 508th by Barbara Cartland.

BARBARA CARTLAND

The Dare-Devil Duke

Mandarin

A Mandarin Paperback
THE DARE-DEVIL DUKE

First published in Great Britain 1996
by Mandarin Paperbacks
an imprint of Reed International Books Ltd
Michelin House, 81 Fulham Road, London SW3 6RB
and Auckland, Melbourne, Singapore and Toronto

Copyright © Cartland Promotions 1996
The author has asserted her moral rights

A CIP catalogue record for this title
is available from the British Library
ISBN 0 7493 1272 6

Printed and bound in Great Britain
by Cox & Wyman Ltd, Reading, Berks.

AUTHOR'S NOTE

'Dare-Devil' is described in Roget's Thesaurus as Knight, a Paladin, Stout Fellow, a Desperado, a Beau Sabreur, Man of Metal, Game-Dog, Bull-Dog, Risk Taker, Fire Eater and a Hero.

Some of the latter are Hector, Achilles, Hotspur, Sir Galahad, Great Heart, Hercules and Don Quixote.

Also included are those receiving the Military Cross for Gallantry, the George Cross and the Victoria Cross.

One of my Grandfather's Uncles was Captain Treweeke Scobell, who had served in the Navy at the Battle of Trafalgar. When he retired he represented Bath in The House Of Commons.

During the Crimean War he tabled a Motion that a medal, which could be worn by both Officers and men, irrespective of rank, should be struck to commemorate outstanding acts of gallantry.

The Government was greatly interested and Queen Victoria was approached to approve the suggestion.

Captain Scobell was then asked to withdraw his Motion and let the idea be brought forward by the Crown. In 1856 the Victoria Cross was instituted by Royal Warrant.

CHAPTER ONE

The Duke yawned.

"I should be leaving."

A soft scented body moved beside him.

"Oh, no, darling," a seductive voice protested. "You cannot leave me so soon. I cannot lose you!"

There appeared to be nothing in her voice that was unusual.

Yet suddenly the Duke was aware of danger.

It was by relying on his exceptional powers of intuition that he had survived to earn the reputation for being a Dare-Devil.

He had undertaken when he was in the Army, what seemed impossible assignments which no other Officer would risk.

When Darcy Horne had come into the title unexpectedly, he had to resign from his Regiment.

He left with a number of medals and honours which were the outward and visible sign of his dashing reputation.

It was his intuition – what he thought of at times as a 'warning voice' – which had kept him alive. It had preserved him to inherit the Dukedom, following the death in action of both of his cousins.

Now, for no reason he could put his finger on, he knew that he must leave.

He rose from the bed despite two clinging arms, and Lady Julie said again:

"Do not go, I beg you, darling, not to leave me. It is far too early!"

"I am tired, Julie," the Duke answered, "and as I have a long day tomorrow, I need my 'Beauty Sleep'!"

He had his back to her as he spoke, and yet he was convinced she looked at the clock.

"It is too early, darling," she said again, "and you know how precious the hours I spend with you are to me."

The Duke started to put on his clothes.

He dressed himself swiftly and with an expertise which always infuriated his Valet.

When he had finished arranging his cravat, he moved back towards the bed.

As he did so, without its occupant being aware of it, he turned the key of the door in the lock and put it into his pocket.

It was a swift movement and done so neatly that Lady Julie had no idea it had happened.

Instead, looking incredibly lovely with her long hair falling over her shoulders, she held out her arms.

The Duke was well aware that if he kissed her, as she intended, she would pull him down on top of her.

Then it would be difficult to escape.

Instead he kissed her hands, one after the other, and said:

"Thank you, Julie. I have enjoyed this evening, and you are very beautiful."

He crossed the room towards a curtain which concealed the wash-hand basin and Julie's elaborate brushes and bottles.

These were the accessories with which she made herself one of the most striking and acclaimed Beauties in the *Beau Monde*.

"What are you doing, Darcy?" she cried as the Duke pulled back the curtain.

The bedroom in the tall, narrow house on the corner of Charles Street and the Mews behind the houses on that side of Berkeley Square had two windows.

One looked out onto Charles Street, and the other, which was hidden by the curtain, onto the Mews behind the houses.

The Duke was aware of this and did not answer.

He thought even as he moved back the curtain that he heard the sound of wheels stopping outside the front of the house.

"What are you doing?" Lady Julie asked again plaintively as the Duke opened the window which overlooked the Mews.

Again he made no reply.

With the agility of an acrobat, he swung himself down from the window-sill and dropped onto the roof of the floor below.

It was easy to scramble from there into the cobbled yard.

Even as he did so he heard someone rattling the door which would not open.

He walked swiftly down the Mews.

When he got to the far end of it, he threw the key that was in his pocket into some bushes.

He then had only a few yards to go to reach his own house in Berkeley Square.

When he did so he told himself he had had a lucky escape.

He had known that Lady Julie's husband Timothy Barlow was hard up.

But he had not thought he would stoop to such an age-old trick as coming back unexpectedly to find his wife in another man's arms.

There were only two options open to the victim.

To fight a duel which might result in his having to live abroad for several years, or to pay up.

The Duke knew that there was no question about what Timothy Barlow would demand.

He would have to pay up rather than be involved in a scandal.

It would be unthinkable so soon after he had inherited his title and the vast Estates that for centuries had belonged to the Dukes of Dreghorne.

"I have had a lucky escape!" he said again.

He knew it was thanks to his intuition which had saved him dozens of times before.

The night-footman sprang to his feet when he heard the knock.

Having let his Master into the house, he shut the door and bolted it.

"Tell Jenkins in the morning," the Duke said, "that I will leave immediately after breakfast for the country."

"Very good, Your Grace," the night-footman murmured.

The Duke walked slowly up the stairs.

Only when he reached his bedroom did he ask himself why the sort of thing that had just happened so often happened to him.

He had found Lady Julie fascinating.

She was also in his opinion, one of the most beautiful women he had ever seen.

The daughter of a Marquess, she had eloped with Timothy Barlow a few days before her seventeenth birthday.

It had been a mistake, though they had in fact, stayed together.

Timothy was a gambler, and there were times when they both wondered where the next penny was coming from.

The Duke could understand that he was the obvious person to solve their problems.

What annoyed him was that he had thought Julie was genuinely infatuated with him.

When he was an unimportant and obviously impecunious soldier, a great number of women had laid their hearts at his feet.

It seemed ironic that now he was a Duke Julie had been more interested in his money than in him.

It was not really that he minded so much parting with thousands of pounds.

It was the humiliation of being caught in a compromising situation against which he had no defence.

At any rate, he thought, it had taught him

a lesson – not to be so conceited in the future.

Also, for the moment, to waste no more of his valuable time in London.

There was, he knew, a great deal for him to do in the country.

The late Duke had been a very old man when he died and had neglected the Estate by not modernising it in any way.

It was not only that the equipment on the farms was out of date.

Most of the horses in the stables were on their last legs.

Quite a number of the servants at the Castle should have been pensioned off years earlier.

The war had of course contributed to that because the young men were away fighting Napoleon, and many of them had not returned.

The Duke knew that he had to bring the Dreghorne Estate up to date.

He had also to restore and preserve the treasures in the Castle which had been handed down from generation to generation.

"The sooner I get to work, the better!" the Duke told himself as he got into bed.

Without another thought for the woman he had just left in an ignominious position behind a locked door, he fell asleep.

. . . .

In the morning, the Duke rang for his Valet before the man called him.

"I 'ears as we're goin' to the country, Yer Grace,"

Bates said when he answered the bell.

"I want to leave before nine o'clock," the Duke said.

"I thought that's wot Yer Grace'd want," Bates answered, "an' Mr. Ashton's sent a groom ahead an hour ago to warn 'em."

The Duke did not reply.

He was used to the excellent way in which his Secretary ran the house.

He knew that Mr. Bennett his counterpart at the Castle would therefore have everything ready when he arrived.

He dressed quickly.

Then he went down to breakfast in the Dining-Room which overlooked the Berkeley Square garden.

Beside his plate were a number of letters that his Secretary had left unopened.

The Duke glanced at them and knew they were mostly *billets-doux* from women who were attracted by him.

"And not only," he told himself cynically, "because they want me to bed them!"

He thought now that last night had taught him a lesson which he would not forget in a hurry.

When next a woman enticed him with an invitation in her eyes, he would question what she really wanted before he succumbed to her beauty.

At the same time he was laughing at himself for coldly analysing anything that was so enjoyable.

He had thanked his lucky stars a million times already for the amazing position which he now occupied.

He had expected to grow old as a serving Officer.

He had reached the rank of Major by the time he left the Army.

But without another war taking place he knew it might be many years before he reached any higher rank.

The war had provided him with many uncomfortable, frightening and certainly dangerous moments.

At the same time it had been a challenge.

He had enjoyed the risks he had taken, simply because he had always been triumphant.

He knew that his Commanding Officers had, even as they praised him, regarded him as a Dare-Devil who would doubtless, sooner or later, come to an untimely end.

It had amused him to see the astonishment on their faces when he and the men he had led returned alive.

What was more, often unscathed from some extraordinarily risky action against the enemy.

He knew that on many occasions the betting had been ten to one against his survival.

And yet he had survived.

Now there was peace and the enemies he was facing were dilapidation, neglect and, worst of all, apathy.

The Duke finished his breakfast before he touched the letters in front of him.

He opened three and tore them up.

They were from women who were hunting him, he told himself, as if he were a fox.

The others were Social invitations, and needed

formal answers which could be dealt with by his secretary.

Letters beseeching him to come to a dinner, a Ball, or a Reception because the hostess wanted to flaunt him in the face of her rivals, he put on one side.

He rang the silver bell that was on the table in front of him.

The Butler answered his summons almost immediately.

"Ask Mr. Ashton to join me in the Study," the Duke said.

"Very good, Your Grace," Jenkins answered, "and when will Your Grace be returning from the country?"

"I have no idea," the Duke replied, "but possibly sooner than you expect."

"I assure Your Grace that whenever it is, we'll be ready for Your Grace's arrival," Jenkins said promptly.

The Duke gave a short laugh.

"I will believe that when I see it!"

Picking up the letters he had set to one side, he went from the room.

He was aware as he did so that Jenkins was looking at him with an expression of admiration in his eyes.

He could not help knowing that all his servants admired him.

This was because Bates had regaled them with stories of his adventures during the war.

As Bates had taken part in many of them, the

Duke was sure he had exaggerated much of what had happened.

At the same time it was pleasingly flattering.

He knew only too well that the housemaids regarded him as a hero.

The male staff would follow him in the same way that his soldiers had done wherever he led them.

As he was giving instructions to Ashton to cancel his engagements for the next few days, the Duke signed a large number of letters and several cheques.

"Will Your Grace be inviting any guests to the country?" Mr. Ashton asked.

The Duke shook his head.

"Not for the moment, but if I want any of my friends to join me, I will send a groom to you with their names."

"I am sure they will be only too delighted to receive any invitation Your Grace may wish to extend to them," Mr. Ashton said.

"That may be," the Duke replied. "However, I have a lot to do, as you well know, Ashton, not only at the Castle, but also on the Estate, which has been sadly neglected."

"I was afraid that is what Your Grace would find," Mr. Ashton said apologetically, "but I know the staff have been doing their best."

The Duke nodded. He was aware of this too.

He left the Study and went into the hall.

From one footman he took his top-hat, from another his gloves.

Outside his Travelling Phaeton, drawn by four horses, was waiting.

He had purchased the team the day after he had come to London on his accession to the title.

He had known that if he had to travel regularly between Berkeley Square and the Castle, he could not bear to be on the road longer than was necessary.

He had already managed to break all records by reaching the Castle in just over two hours.

He was determined he would improve on that before he was satisfied.

He climbed into the driving-seat.

The groom who usually accompanied him jumped up onto the seat behind.

The staff who were standing on the steps bowed as he gathered up the reins.

The Duke raised his whip in a salute before he drove off.

As he did so he felt a sudden thrill of delight which was more intense than anything he had felt last night.

The team he had picked out at Tattersall's Sale Rooms was outstanding.

He learned they were for sale only because their owner had died.

The Trustees of his Estate were working on behalf of a boy of twelve, and saw no point in keeping them.

The Duke had in fact paid a large sum for them, as he was not the only bidder.

Now he thought they were worth every penny of what they had cost him.

He tooled his Phaeton through what traffic there was on the roads leading down to the River and then to the South.

Then they were in the open countryside and he gave his team their heads.

As they moved with remarkable swiftness, he thought to drive them was the most enjoyable thing he had done for a long time.

As the Duke left his house in Berkeley Square, on the opposite side of the Square Sir Roland Ross was looking out of the window.

His house was on the corner of Bruton Street.

It annoyed him that the Duke's team was more impressive than his own, although he had paid a very large sum of money for his bays.

If there was one thing Sir Roland disliked, it was that a younger man had surpassed him in business, in sport, or in his possessions.

Immensely rich, he had made his millions himself.

He was therefore contemptuous of those who had, regardless of merit simply inherited their wealth and their position.

He had been made a Knight three years ago after giving vast contributions to the Whigs.

In fact, they were so large that he often thought angrily that his Knighthood had cost him too much.

As he watched the Duke drive out of the Square he asked himself what he could do about his daughter Kasia.

Yesterday, in this very room in which he was now standing, she had defied him.

He had sent for her and she came obediently.

He had thought as she appeared that she was very lovely.

In fact she closely resembled her Mother, whom Sir Roland missed every minute of the day.

Lady Margaret had been only a month or so older than his daughter was now, when she first saw Roland Ross.

He was an extremely handsome young man, but of no social importance.

His Father was Vicar of a Parish on the estate of the Earl of Malford.

Roland had met Lady Margaret at a Bazaar arranged by the Vicar and his wife.

The proceeds of which were to repair the Church Tower.

It had taken them only a few hours before they fell in love.

When the Earl of Malford heard about it, he was furious.

He forbade his daughter to see Roland again and threatened to throw the Vicar out of his Living.

The two young people however did not listen.

They eloped romantically, which enraged the Earl.

He almost struck the Vicar when he admitted that he could not control his son.

He also predicted that the young couple would starve.

Only when they were in rags and begging his forgiveness would he take his daughter back into the family.

None of those things had happened.

Roland and his young bride went to Liverpool

where he became involved in the Shipping industry.

In a series of extraordinary circumstances and also because he was very intelligent, he was more or less adopted by a most successful Ship-owner.

As he had no son, when he died he left Roland his ships and his business.

From that moment, or really from the moment he married Margaret, Roland climbed to the top.

By the time his wife died he was enormously wealthy.

He had only worked so that he could lay his millions at her feet and prove himself worthy of her.

Now there was no need for him to go on accumulating more and more wealth.

Because Lady Margaret had never been very strong, they had only one child, who had been christened Kasia.

It was an unusual name, but it meant 'Pure' in Polish.

Because Roland was doing some business with that country at the moment of her birth it seemed appropriate.

Kasia had the best Governesses and Tutors obtainable.

For the last two years she had been at the most important and selective Academy for young Ladies in Bath.

She was to make her debut this season and Sir Roland had already arranged an enormous ball for her.

It was to take place at the end of May.

First she must be presented at Buckingham Palace to The Queen and The Prince Consort.

Sir Roland was even more excited about it than she was.

"You shall have the most beautiful and the most expensive gown that any debutante has ever owned," he said a dozen times.

"I do not suppose anyone will notice me, Papa," Kasia replied, "when there are so many other girls being presented, and it seems extravagant when I have so many gowns already, which I have not yet worn."

"You will do as I tell you!" Sir Roland thundered.

When the Presentation took place he was upset.

Although her name was reported in Court Circulars, they said little about Kasia except that she was his daughter.

Other debutantes of course, because they were the daughters of Dukes and Marquesses, had several lines written about them.

In some cases their gowns were described in detail.

Sir Roland was very scathing about the partiality of newspapers.

Kasia, however, had merely laughed.

"You will have to get yourself a Dukedom, Papa," she said.

"I could buy the newspaper, for that matter!" Sir Roland muttered.

Kasia laughed again.

"No, no, Papa, you possess enough already, and you know the Doctor said you were not to do as much as you have been doing."

"If you are worrying about me," Sir Roland said, "it is quite unnecessary. I am well enough to look after you, and I know what are your rights."

Kasia had kissed his cheek.

He was still a very handsome man, but she knew that, obsessed by his own importance, he was determined always to have his own way.

It was a week later that the blow fell.

Kasia had gone into the garden in Berkeley Square to meet a friend.

A footman came hurrying into the Square to say that her Father wanted her.

"I will come at once," Kasia said.

She kissed her friend good-bye who had her Chaperon with her, and hurried back to the house.

Sir Roland was in his Study which, not surprisingly, had some fine pictures of ships on the walls.

"Ah, here you are, my dearest," he said when Kasia came in. "I wondered where you were."

"I was in the garden, Papa," Kasia replied, "and we have no engagement for luncheon."

"That is good, very good!" Sir Roland approved.

"Why?" Kasia asked.

There was some hesitation before Sir Roland replied:

"I want to tell you, my dearest, that I have chosen a husband for you."

"Chosen a husband for me!" Kasia exclaimed. "What do you mean?"

"I mean what I say," Sir Roland replied. "I have been worried, very worried, my dear, that you

26

would be married for your money. You see, when I die, you will be enormously rich."

He paused and his voice deepened.

"I could not bear that you should marry some Ne'er-do-well who will throw what I have made into the gutter, or gamble it away on the turn of a card, as happens so often in the Clubs."

Kasia stared at him. Then she said:

"I . . I do not understand what . . you are . . saying."

"I am saying," Sir Roland replied, "that Lord Stefelton, for whom I have the greatest respect, and who has an intelligent and well-balanced brain, wishes you to become his wife, and I have given my consent."

Kasia looked at her Father as if she could not find words to answer him.

Her Father looked at her impatiently and she said at last:

"N.no, Papa! Of course I would . . not marry . . someone I do not . . love! I have met Lord Stefelton, but it never crossed my mind for a moment that you would want me to . . marry a man who is so much older than I am . . and whom I hardly know."

"I have already told you," Sir Roland said, "that Stefelton has an excellent brain. He will handle your fortune as I would wish him to do, and will certainly not fritter it away as some young idiot would."

Kasia was aware that her Father had been upset by reports of how the Bucks and *Beaux* had nothing better to do than wager thousands of pounds on which fly reached the top of the window-pane first.

"I am sorry, Papa," she said in a quiet voice, "but although I love you, I will . . not allow you to . . choose my husband for me . . just as Mama chose you . . despite what her Father said . . so as she did . . I will choose . . the man I . . love."

"You will do nothing of the sort!" Sir Roland said sharply. "Your Mother and I, in running away, were fortunate that things turned out so well. But I have since thought that it was a very dangerous thing to do, and something I would never allow my own daughter to contemplate."

"What you are saying, Papa, is that you will not allow me to marry somebody I love. That means I will have to elope . . as you and Mama did."

"You will do nothing of the sort!" Sir Roland repeated angrily. "Where you are concerned, things are very different. You are a great heiress, and I do not believe there is a man alive who would not be influenced by that!"

"Then of course, I must remain unmarried," Kasia replied.

"Do not talk such nonsense!" Sir Roland snapped. "Of course you must marry. You must have children to inherit your wealth. If it were possible, I would like to have had a dozen sons of my own."

"I think you are being greedy," Kasia said. "I have never known two people happier than you and Mama were."

Sir Roland's eyes softened.

"That is true, but it is something that happens once in a million times, and, as I have already said, where you are concerned, it is different."

"I cannot see the difference," Kasia retorted. "Quite frankly, Papa, I will not marry any man I do not love. And if you refuse to give me any money, then I will have to fend for myself."

Her Father laughed scornfully.

"Do you really think you could work as I had to work to keep your Mother from starvation? My dear child, you have lived in the lap of luxury all your life. You could no more earn a penny piece than fly over the moon!"

There was silence.

Then Kasia said:

"Whether that is true or not, I assure you, Papa, that never will I marry Lord Stefelton!"

She turned as she spoke and walked out of the Study.

As she shut the door quietly behind her, Sir Roland thumped angrily with his closed fist on the writing-table.

CHAPTER TWO

Kasia went to the Drawing-Room where she had always sat with her Mother.

She stood at the window looking out sightlessly onto the Square.

How was it possible that her Father should behave like this?

She was determined not to do what he wanted; at the same time she was afraid.

She was well aware that her Father had not got to the top without being utterly and completely determined and often ruthless.

She had always thought it very romantic that he had worked so arduously simply because he loved his wife.

He was determined that she should have everything that she had sacrificed by marrying him.

The only person who could do anything with Sir Roland was his wife.

Kasia could remember how cleverly her Mother would coax him.

Whether into giving her something she wanted, or doing something he did not want to do.

She knew that she could not do the same.

'If only . . Mama were . . alive,' she thought desperately, 'she would stop him behaving in this . . horrible manner.'

She could in a way understand her Father's feelings.

He had built up his empire by his own endeavours.

He was therefore afraid that it would be wasted or destroyed when he was dead.

Because Kasia was agitated she walked backwards and forwards across the carpet.

She felt she might lose her self-control.

She might start wringing her hands helplessly in Eastern fashion.

Then she told herself that she was her Father's daughter.

She had the brains to defeat him in this crisis and must use them.

"What can . . I do? What . . can I . . do?" she asked over and over again.

He had said she was incapable of earning her own living.

She could hear the mockery in his voice when he said:

"You could no more earn a penny piece than fly over the moon!"

'If that is true,' Kasia thought, 'then why have I studied so hard and for so long and come home with every possible prize?'

She had felt very proud of herself when she had returned from Bath.

She had been top of her class in five subjects.

Now as she thought of it, she remembered that her Father had not been as overwhelmed by her success as she had hoped.

"Very good, my dear," he said, "and now we must start planning what you will wear when you are presented at Buckingham Palace."

"I have a good brain, of course I have!" Kasia said now. "So I have to prove to him that he is wrong, and that I am capable of standing on my own two feet and choosing my own husband!"

She walked across the room again.

As she did so, she noticed the newspapers lying on a stool in front of the fireplace.

Those which had interested her Mother were still always laid out there.

The financial newspapers were always arranged in her Father's Study.

Kasia picked up the *Morning Post*, not feeling very hopeful.

She knew there were 'Wanted' advertisements.

Perhaps there might be something there which would be of help to her.

She sent up a little prayer not only to God but also to her Mother.

"Help me, Mama, help me! You know Papa is wrong, but he will not listen to me in the way he listened to you. You . . must help . . me!"

She had hardly said the words when she saw directly in front of her the 'Wanted' column.

There was a paragraph with at the bottom of it an address in Berkeley Square.

It was the address that caught her eye.

As she read the paragraph she knew that her Mother must have guided her, for it read:

"WANTED: Young Governess for boy of seven. Apply: The Secretary, 29 Berkeley Square, London."

As she read it two or three times, she was aware that the number marked was on the other side of the Square.

She put down the *Morning Post*, and went into the hall.

She picked up her bonnet which she had placed on a chair when she had come in hastily from the garden.

As a footman opened the front door for her she said:

"If the Master wants me, tell him I have gone to rejoin my friend in the Square."

"Very good, Miss Kasia," the footman said.

As Kasia ran down the steps she was well aware that her friend and her Chaperon would have left by now.

As she unlocked the gate into the garden, she saw with relief that there was no one there.

She had therefore no difficulty in walking to the other side and opening the gate with the residents' key.

When she had been at School in Bath, she had always spent the holidays in her Father's house in the country.

She had therefore little idea of who lived in the other houses in Berkeley Square.

As she knocked on the door of No. 29 she was aware there was an impressive crest on the silver knocker.

The door was opened immediately and she said to the footman:

"I have come in answer to the advertisement."

For a moment he looked surprised, then as if he remembered he said:

"I'll take you t' Mr. Ashton, Ma'am."

He shut the door and went ahead of her down a long passage.

At the end of it the footman knocked on the door and opened it.

"A lady t' see you, Sir," he announced.

Kasia realised immediately that she was being shown into the Secretary's Room.

The man sitting at the desk was obviously Secretary to the owner of the house.

He was a middle-aged man with rather tired eyes.

When he looked up at her he rose to his feet.

"I have seen your advertisement," Kasia said, "and I would like to apply for the position you are advertising."

"Will you sit down?" Mr. Ashton invited.

He indicated a chair on the other side of his desk.

Kasia did so.

A quick glance round the room told her that whoever was the owner of the house was a man of some importance.

There were maps on the walls which depicted a large estate.

There was also what looked like an old oil painting of a Castle.

She thought that the Secretary was looking at her a little critically.

He might be thinking that her clothes were too expensive for those of a Governess.

Actually Mr. Ashton was thinking that the first applicant for the position he had advertised was far too pretty and too young.

A young girl was nevertheless what he had stipulated, and picking up his pen he said:

"Perhaps we should start by your telling me your name?"

Kasia had already thought of this as she was crossing the Square.

"It is Watson," she said, "Kate Watson."

It was the name of one of her Governesses, and she felt it certainly sounded suitable.

"You have had some experience in teaching?" Mr. Ashton asked.

Kasia thought it was better to tell the truth.

"I am afraid not," she said, "but I have been very well educated. I speak both French and Italian, and I have won prizes in most subjects in my School curriculum."

Mr. Ashton wrote this down. Then he said:

"The situation I am offering, Miss Watson, is a difficult one."

"Difficult?" Kasia queried.

"I think I should be honest and say *very* difficult!"

Mr. Ashton admitted. "And I should tell you too that although I advertised for someone young, I was not expecting someone quite as young as yourself."

Quickly Kasia replied:

"I am not as young as I look. In fact I am nearly twenty-one."

It was not the truth.

But Kasia thought if she could obtain this position and earn her living it would teach her Father a lesson.

Also, if anything went wrong, it would be easy to return home immediately.

Mr. Ashton wrote down her name and her age. Then he said:

"In which case, you may be able to cope with the pupil for whom I am trying to find a Governess."

"You mean the little boy of seven," Kasia said. "Why is he so difficult?"

"That is the unanswered question," Mr. Ashton replied. "He is very difficult indeed!"

There was a pause, then when Kasia did not speak, he said:

"I presume you know to whom this house belongs?"

"I have no idea," Kasia replied truthfully.

"It belongs to the Duke of Dreghorne, who has recently come into the title," Mr. Ashton explained. "His uncle, the late Duke, was very old and had been ill for some years before he died."

Kasia was listening carefully.

"Is this the little boy who needs a Governess," she asked, "the miser Duke's son?"

36

"No, his nephew," Mr. Ashton replied. "The child's Father was killed during the war and his Mother died shortly afterwards."

"So he is an orphan," Kasia murmured.

"Quite so, Miss Watson, and that is what underlies the problem."

Kasia looked at him enquiringly, and he explained:

"He has been sent to live with one relative after another, none of whom I gather really wanted him. He has therefore been, as one might put it, 'homeless' for some years. He has finally been sent to Dreghorne Castle because nobody else will have him."

"And the Castle is in the country, I suppose?"

"Yes, Miss Watson, and the boy's last Tutor whom I chose for him has left, saying that the child is impossible and he will waste no more time in trying to teach him anything."

"That sounds rather feeble," Kasia remarked.

This was something Mr. Ashton was not expecting and he gave a little laugh.

"I might have thought that myself, Miss Watson, had not a number of Governesses and Tutors before him said the same thing."

"The little boy is not . . insane . . is he?" Kasia asked.

Mr. Ashton shook his head.

"No, indeed, he is certainly not that. It is just that he refuses to learn, and takes a violent dislike to all his Tutors."

"You say he has had a number of them, so I

can understand that," Kasia said. "Perhaps I will succeed where everybody else has failed."

"Are you really willing to undertake such a difficult task?" Mr. Ashton asked.

There was a note of surprise in his voice.

Kasia was sure he had assumed that when he told her the truth she would no longer be interested.

"Shall I say," Kasia said slowly, "that I would like to take a chance on it."

She realised that Mr. Ashton was looking at her speculatively and she said quickly:

"I am very anxious to find work immediately, and it would suit me if I could go to the Castle tomorrow."

Mr. Ashton drew in his breath.

"I think, Miss Watson, I would be correct in asking for references or credentials."

"Yes, of course," Kasia agreed, "and I know that Lady Margaret Ross who lived in the Square, would have given me one, if she had not died a year ago."

She paused a moment and then went on:

"There is also the Countess of Malford, to whom I am distantly related, but she unfortunately lives in Derbyshire, and that would take rather a long time."

Kasia had in fact, never met the Countess of Malford, her grandmother, although her Mother had often talked about her.

She thought however, she could forge references without Mr. Ashton suspecting anything.

The last time her Mother had spoken of the

Countess she was then nearly eighty, and not in particularly good health.

Mr. Ashton was obviously impressed, but at the same time still thinking he should have a reference.

There was a somewhat uncomfortable pause.

Then he asked:

"There is no one else you know of, Miss Watson, who would vouch for you?"

"There are plenty of people who would inform you that I am hard working and, I hope, intelligent," Kasia replied, "but I am not sure that all of them are in 'Debrett's Peerage'!"

Mr. Ashton laughed.

"I will tell you what I will do, Miss Watson," he said. "Having seen you and talked to you, I too will take a chance and send you to the Castle."

He smiled at Kasia and then continued:

"His Grace's Secretary there, Mr. Bennett, will be extremely grateful if I can supply someone immediately, and I know you will do your best to look after Master Simon until we can find someone a little older."

Kasia thought that would suit her very well.

She was certain her Father would be extremely agitated on finding she had left home.

But he would eventually capitulate over her marriage to Lord Stefelton. Then she could return.

"Can I leave tomorrow?" she asked.

"Certainly, if you will tell me where the travelling-carriage which will take you to the Castle can pick you up," Mr. Ashton replied.

Kasia gave him the address of a friend of hers who lived in Islington Square.

It was a girl with whom she had been friends at School, and whom she had heard from only this morning.

She had written her a letter saying that she hoped to see her while she was in London, but she was at the moment laid up having sprained her ankle.

Mr. Ashton was noting down the address.

"What time would suit you?" he asked. "I must tell you that it takes about three hours to reach the Castle."

Kasia thought quickly.

She was certain her Father would leave the house as he usually did at about nine o'clock.

He nearly always had Board Meetings to attend in the City.

"I can be ready by ten o'clock," she said.

"That means you will arrive at the Castle in time for luncheon," Mr. Ashton said, "and I will send a groom first thing in the morning to tell Mr. Bennett to expect you."

"Thank you, thank you very much," Kasia said, "and I promise you I will do my best. However, if I fail, I am sure you will understand."

"I have been frank with you," Mr. Ashton said, "and although I shall be disappointed, Miss Watson, if you do fail, I shall just have to try again."

He spoke philosophically, and Kasia said:

"I can only say that I will do everything I can."

She rose as she spoke and held out her hand.

Mr. Ashton looked up at her in surprise.

"Have you not forgotten something rather important, Miss Watson?"

"What is that?" Kasia enquired.

"We have not discussed your wages."

"Nor we have! I quite forgot!"

"It is something that most people consider of more importance than anything else," Mr. Ashton said. "Your wages will be paid weekly, or monthly, whichever you prefer and the Duke is a generous man."

"I think weekly would be more convenient," Kasia replied. "If as you say, the Duke is generous, I will accept what he thinks is appropriate."

Mr. Ashton made a note of this before he rose to his feet.

He walked to the door and opened it for Kasia.

"I can only say, Miss Watson," he said, "that you are unlike any Governess I have ever engaged before, and you have raised my hopes."

"Then I must try not to dash them!" Kasia replied.

She was not surprised, because he was obviously intrigued by her unusual application, that he walked with her to the front door.

She had however, no wish for him to see her go across into the garden.

She therefore shook hands with him and walked away quickly down the street.

She had the feeling that a little uncertainly he was still watching her.

She therefore deliberately walked round the Square to her Father's house.

The trees in the garden would prevent him from seeing her after she had turned the first corner.

To make absolutely certain of being unseen she slipped down to the basement.

She waited there outside the kitchen-door for some minutes.

Then she walked back up again and knocked for the footman to open the front door.

Once in the hall she asked:

"Is the Master in his Study?"

"No, Miss Kasia," the footman replied. "He's gone out."

That was what Kasia had hoped and she went upstairs to her bedroom.

She and her Father were dining tonight with a hostess who was giving a Ball for her debutante daughter.

Kasia was determined not to be ready until they were actually expected at the dinner-party.

She thought her Father could hardly start fighting with her in the carriage when they had only a short distance to go.

"I will have breakfast in bed tomorrow, Molly," she said to her lady's-maid, "but I would like it at eight o'clock."

"Isn't that too early for you, Miss?" the lady's-maid enquired. "You'll be tired after dancin' all night."

"I do not intend to be late tonight," Kasia answered, "and as my Father is accompanying me, he is certain to want to come home early."

This was true.

Sir Roland enjoyed seeing the success his daughter was at the parties and Balls to which she was invited.

But he continually looked at his watch, and seeing him as she danced past always made Kasia feel guilty.

Tonight, she thought, she might have made the most of the Ball.

It would be the last one she would go to for some time.

But she knew she had a lot to do in the morning, if the Duke's carriage was to call for her at ten o'clock at her friend's house in Islington.

When she went downstairs her Father was waiting for her.

Although she did not realise it, she was looking very beautiful in one of her new debutante gowns.

She was sure that, not having seen her since she walked out of his Study, he assumed he had won the battle.

He would have told himself that she had seen sense.

He would have assumed she was leaving it to him to arrange her future life as he had arranged everything else for her up until now.

"Do you like my new gown, Papa?" Kasia asked as she walked into the room.

"You look lovely, my dearest," he replied, "and so very like your Mother."

There was a note of pain in his voice which made Kasia feel sorry for him.

Just for a moment she thought it was wrong of her to cause him anxiety.

But she was determined to save herself from what she knew would be abject misery in being married to a man she disliked.

It was something she kept thinking about, although she tried not to, all through the evening.

Fortunately Lord Stefelton was not at the party.

Kasia kept comparing him to the young men who asked her to dance.

They were all very much younger than he was, which was at least in his early forties.

He was, she thought, almost as ambitious as her Father had been at the same age.

She knew he would be delighted at the prospect of being involved in the business in which Roland Ross had been such a success.

Kasia could appreciate that he was clever.

At the same time she had found him unattractive as a man.

He had, she told herself, cold eyes.

Every instinct in her body shrank from the idea of him touching her.

As she danced she kept asking herself how her Father, who had been so wildly in love with her Mother, could force her into a loveless marriage.

Especially with a man who she suspected was not particularly in love with her.

She was, moreover, well aware that her Father was still a very handsome man.

He was also enormously rich and the Ladies present were all fawning over him and flattering him.

Almost despite himself he was enjoying it.

Kasia thought he must be blind, deaf and dumb to think she would accept a man for whom she had no feeling at all.

Yet, she was sensitive enough to realise what his enormous fortune meant to her Father.

The foundation of it he had built up pound by pound as it were.

Then on inheriting the shipping business, which he had already helped to make prosperous, he had multiplied and multiplied it until his fortune was like a mountain of gold that he must preserve at all costs.

"That, of course, means sacrificing me!" Kasia thought desperately, and she was no longer sorry for him.

When they drove home together at one o'clock in the morning, she deliberately talked of the party.

"You were a huge success, Papa!" she said. "I saw all those beautiful women making eyes at you!"

"If they did, I did not notice them," her Father said hastily. "You know, Kasia, no one could ever compare with your Mother."

"All the same, I think Mama would want you to enjoy yourself," Kasia said. "She always thought you worked too hard, and now you cannot possibly want to be richer than you are already!"

"I want to be rich for you and your children," Sir Roland answered.

Kasia thought, if she had the children he envisaged, they would also be Lord Stefelton's and she shuddered.

45

"You are going too fast, Papa," she said, "and I have not had my Ball yet."

"It is going to be the best Ball of the Season!" Sir Roland said in a confident voice. "And everyone will talk about it afterwards."

There was a little pause and he said:

"All I want you to do, my dearest, is to let me announce your engagement to Stefelton. After that, the fortune-hunters will keep away."

"I am too tired to talk about it tonight, Papa," Kasia said rather sleepily.

"Yes, yes, of course," Sir Roland agreed. "I am going to the City in the morning, but we will have luncheon together, unless of course you have a previous engagement."

"I have really forgotten," Kasia said, "but I expect I shall be awake by then."

She kissed her Father goodnight in the hall and hurried up the stairs.

She knew he would go first to his Study, to see if there were any messages for him on his desk.

As Kasia got into bed, she told herself that the evening had passed off better than she had anticipated.

She could only pray that nothing would go wrong tomorrow.

"I know that Papa is completely and utterly determined that I shall marry Lord Stefelton," she told herself, "and I am completely and utterly determined that I will not! We shall just have to see who wins."

Kasia was called, as she had ordered, at eight o'clock.

As soon as she had eaten her breakfast, she got out of bed and started taking from the wardrobe the most simple of her gowns.

She hoped they were not too unsuitable in her position as a Governess.

She knew however, that the average Governess could not have afforded even one of them.

But she thought, if she was asked, she would simply say that she had been given them by a wealthy friend.

At the same time, she was aware that the Duke of Dreghorne was not married.

If there was no woman at the Castle, she would not be bothered by tiresome questions, or awkward suspicions.

She remembered hearing about the Duke from some of the girls at the luncheons she had attended.

Her Father had managed to get her invited by the Mothers of other debutantes to luncheons and tea-parties at which only the young were present.

Kasia actually found them rather boring.

She listened to what they talked about and found to her surprise it consisted of a great deal of gossip.

They discussed their Mothers, and the well known Beauties of the *Beau Monde*.

They quoted their brothers and their Fathers in citing who was more beautiful than anyone else.

They also talked in low whispers about all the

notorious *affaires de coeur* in the *Beau Monde*.

At one of these parties Kasia had heard that the Duke of Dreghorne was one of the heroes of the war.

They also said he was closely involved with Lady Julie Barlow.

She was one of the outstanding Beauties whom no man could resist.

Kasia thought she would have liked to see her.

But at the three Balls she had attended up to date, there had been no sign of Lady Julie.

Nor for that matter of the Duke of Dreghorne.

She wondered if there was any chance of their coming to the Castle.

In which case, doubtless as a Governess, she would be able to peep at them over the banisters.

She must also catch a glimpse of them in the garden from one of the upper windows.

She laughed to herself at the idea.

At the same time, she knew she must be very careful to 'keep her place'.

Which was, as far as a Governess was concerned, 'between Heaven and Hell' or more bluntly, 'between the Gentry and the servants'.

She remembered her Mother saying once:

"I always feel sorry for Governesses. They really have a very lonely time."

"Why should you think that, Mama?" Kasia had asked.

"Although they are Ladies, they are not accepted in the Drawing-Room, and they have no wish to be too friendly even with the upper servants," Lady

48

Margaret had said slowly. "I often wonder if with only the chatter of small children to listen to, they do not find it extremely boring."

After that, Kasia had been aware that her Mother was always specially kind to her Governesses.

Sometimes, when it was possible, she included them in the parties she was giving.

"That is my position now," she told herself, "and I must be very careful not to step out of it."

She watched the clock.

When she realised that her Father would have left the house she rang for her lady's-maid.

"I am going to stay with a friend of mine in the country," she said. "Pack all these things quickly, as I have to be at her house at half-past-nine."

"Well, you'll 'ave to 'urry, Miss Kasia," the maid said.

She quickly placed the gowns into a trunk, while Kasia picked out the simplest bonnets she had.

She thought several of them would look more appropriate if she removed the flowers and feathers.

She decided she would do that when she reached the Castle.

It was about twenty minutes past nine when the hackney-carriage she had ordered drew up outside the front door.

"I did not know you were going away, Miss Kasia," the Butler said as she reached the hall.

"It is only for a night or so," Kasia replied. "I am staying with a girl I met last night for a party they are giving in the country."

"I expect the Master has the address?" the Butler questioned.

Kasia pretended she had not heard him.

She hurried down the steps and into the carriage.

She gave the footman the address in Islington.

She thought as she did so that her Father would find it hard to trace her from there.

As they drove away she glanced across the Square in the direction of the Duke's house.

'This is an adventure,' she thought. 'At the same time, I am sure it will make Papa very, very angry!'

CHAPTER THREE

When she left home she had taken with her a present for her friend.

It was a bottle of expensive French Scent she had bought for herself.

She also told the maid at the last minute to collect a large arrangement of Malmaison carnations from a vase in the Drawing-Room.

They were wrapped so that she could present them at the same time.

Her Mother had always taught her that, when she was visiting or staying with anyone, she should always take them a small present.

"It is an Eastern habit," Lady Margaret had said, "which I have always thought was attractive."

'Elizabeth will be pleased to see me,' Kasia thought as she got into the carriage.

Her presents were lying on the opposite seat.

When she arrived at Elizabeth's house she paid the driver and told him not to wait.

She then informed the old manservant that she was being called for in about a quarter of an hour.

"The coachman will ask for a Miss Watson," she said.

"Miss Dobson?" he repeated, holding his hand to his ear.

"That is right!" Kasia said.

She thought if when she was missing, her Father made enquiries the more complicated it was for him, the better.

She was taken up to her friend's room, who was delighted to see her.

"How kind of you to visit me, Kasia," she said, "and thank you . . thank you for the lovely presents."

"I am on my way to the country," Kasia said, "and therefore I cannot stay long, but I will come and see you as soon as I return."

"That would be lovely!" Elizabeth answered. "How pretty you look, and so very smart!"

Kasia thought that was the last thing she should look, in the circumstances.

But there was nothing she could do about it.

She sat and chatted until the old Butler came to tell her that the carriage was outside.

"I must go now, Elizabeth," she said. "Take care of yourself, and do not try to walk too soon."

Elizabeth sighed.

"It was so stupid of me to sprain my ankle just at this moment. It means I cannot go to any Balls."

"I am sure it will be perfectly all right in a week," Kasia said. "I shall be back by then."

She kissed Elizabeth goodbye and wondered as

she went down the stairs if that was the truth.

She had a feeling that her Father might take longer before he capitulated.

In any case she was not certain how she would know if he had.

The carriage waiting for her outside was a Travelling-Chariot.

Although it looked rather old-fashioned she knew with delight it would move at a good pace.

It was drawn by two horses which appeared to be strong and should be swift.

She got into it beside the driver, and the footman who accompanied him sat at the back behind the hood.

As they drove off Kasia said:

"How long do you think it will take?"

"Oi'll do me best, Miss, t'make it as short as is possible," the coachman replied. "These 'orses be th' best we've got in t'stables. But Oi 'ears 'Is Grace be buyin' a great many more which be wot we needs."

Kasia smiled.

She knew coachmen and grooms were never satisfied however many horses they had.

Then she remembered that the Duke had only recently come into the title.

She hoped that when she got to the Castle she would be able to ride.

She had carefully laid out a riding-habit with her dresses.

At the same time she had the uncomfortable suspicion that a Governess was only expected to use a pony-cart.

She did not talk very much as they drove on.

Instead she was thinking how she could make a pupil with such a dismal reputation accept her as his teacher.

She was sure in her mind that he must have been in some way, mishandled.

Otherwise why should he be so hostile to everyone who was in charge of him?

She remembered her Mother saying that all children needed love.

It was those who came from bad homes and dissolute parents that made trouble in the village.

Because the coachman was determined to be as quick as possible, they actually turned in at the Castle gates at a quarter to one.

He was obviously delighted at being quicker than he had anticipated and Kasia congratulated him.

As they drove up the drive she could see the Castle at the end of it.

It was certainly impressive.

Very large, the original Castle must have been added to considerably over the centuries.

Kasia had always been interested in architecture.

She was therefore certain that a new façade had been added in the last century, doubtless by the brothers Adam.

There was a wing on one side and the ancient Castle itself on the other side of a centre block.

Kasia thought it would be fascinating to explore it.

She only hoped she would have a chance to do

so before her employer forced her to keep to the Schoolroom.

As they drew nearer she glanced up at the top of the centre block and saw the pole, but there was no flag.

That told her that the Duke was not in residence and she heaved a sigh of relief.

She had the feeling that he might be difficult about his nephew having anyone so young as a Governess.

They drew up outside the front steps and a footman ran down to open the carriage door.

There was, of course, Kasia noticed, no red carpet where she was concerned.

She walked into the hall and was greeted by a white-haired Butler who said:

"Good day, Miss Watson. We were told to expect you, and Mr. Bennett is waiting to see you in his Office."

He did not wait for her to answer, but walked ahead of her down a long corridor.

It was the same procedure, she thought, that had taken place in Berkeley Square.

The Secretary's room here however, was much larger, and there were many more maps on the walls.

Mr. Bennett was rather like Mr. Ashton, except that he was older.

He rose when she entered and held out his hand.

"I am delighted to see you, Miss Watson," he said politely. "Mr. Ashton informed me that you were arriving, but you are earlier than I expected."

"The horses brought me here very quickly," Kasia explained.

She was aware that the Secretary was looking at her with barely concealed surprise.

She thought that, like Mr. Ashton, he was going to tell her she was too young for the post.

"Will you sit down?" Mr. Bennett suggested.

Kasia sat as he indicated, on an upright chair which was on the other side of his desk.

Mr. Bennett looked down at a letter he held in his hand.

"Mr. Ashton tells me that you are prepared to undertake the education of Master Simon Horne, and that he has explained to you that it is in fact, a very difficult position."

"Mr. Ashton was very frank," Kasia replied. "I told him I would do my best."

"No one can do more, and I am very grateful to you for trying."

He spoke in a somewhat tired manner, as if he did not like to think of the difficulties that lay ahead.

Then Kasia asked:

"What does he do that has upset so many other teachers?"

"Well, with the last one," Mr. Bennett replied, "who was a very intelligent man, the boy took an unreasonable dislike to him, and finally threw an ink-pot which hit him on the chin and drenched his clothes with ink."

Because she could not help it, Kasia laughed.

"I only hope that does not happen to me!"

"I have taken the precaution," Mr. Bennett said,

"of having the ink-pots removed from the School-Room, and have told Master Simon that in future he will use only pencils."

"What did he say to that?" Kasia asked.

"He said he had no intention of learning anything anyway!" Mr. Bennett replied.

"You have prepared me for the worst," Kasia said lightly. "Shall I see him now?"

"I thought you would like first to have some luncheon," Mr. Bennett replied. "Master Simon had his at twelve-thirty in the School-Room, but you might find it more agreeable to eat alone."

"Thank you, that is kind of you," Kasia said.

"I have instructed the Housekeeper, Mrs. Meadows, that you should not use the room which is next to Master Simon's, but another on the same landing, which has a Sitting-Room attached to it."

He hesitated for a moment. Then he said:

"I feel, Miss Watson, you will wish from time to time, to have some rest from your arduous duties, in which case, one of the housemaids will deputise for you."

"Thank you," Kasia said. "You have kindly thought of everything."

She rose as she spoke and Mr. Bennett put up his hand to the bell-pull.

The door opened almost immediately and Kasia was sure the servant had been waiting outside.

"Please take Miss Watson to the room which Mrs. Meadows has assigned to her," he said, "and not to the School-Room."

"Oi knows which it be, Sir," the footman replied.

"Thank you very much," Kasia said as she left the Office.

She was well aware that Mr. Bennett was looking at her with some anxiety, being quite sure, she thought, that she was too young for the position she had taken.

The footman was going ahead of her up a side-staircase.

He obviously thought the same for as they neared the first landing he said:

"Ye've let yerself in fer a real shock, Miss!"

"Why do you say that?" Kasia asked, knowing the answer.

"Th' young gen'man be a real problem, an' no mistake!" the footman answered. "There ain't no one as can do anythin' wiv 'im, an' that's th' truth."

"Perhaps I will prove to be the exception," Kasia said.

"Oi wishes ye Good Luck!" the footman replied, "an' Oi ain't 'alf glad it ain't me!"

He climbed another flight of stairs which took them to the Second Floor.

Then Kasia was led along a passage.

They passed a door which she thought must be the School-Room.

Then some way further along the footman led her into a small, but attractive Sitting-Room.

It was well furnished, and there was a bookcase at one end.

"This be th' room used by th' Companion to 'er late Ladyship," the footman said. "Ever so keen on books, 'er was. They tells Oi th' footman were forever running up an' down t' th' library t' get 'em for 'er."

"I might want the same," Kasia said.

"Ye asks me an' Oi'll fetch ye anythin' ye wants," the footman replied, "an' don't upset yerself if things goes wrong. They ain't never bin right since Oi've bin 'ere."

She thought he was being kind to her, and at the same time admired her.

'At least,' she thought, 'the staff will support me, if no one else will.'

She saw there was a table laid in the centre of the room.

The footman turned towards the door.

"Oi'll tell 'em downstairs ye're ready for yer lunch – oh, an' yer bedroom be yonder."

He pointed to a door at the other end of the room and said:

"If ye wants me, just ask fer Jim."

"I will certainly do that," Kasia said, "and thank you for being so helpful."

"Be a pleasure, Miss," Jim said.

As he reached the door he turned back and winked.

"Keep yer pecker up," he said. "It might not be as bad as yer thinks."

Kasia laughed and went into the bedroom.

She could not imagine any of her Father's servants talking to her in such a familiar way.

But now she was just a Governess.

Jim was not taking liberties, but treating her in a way that was correct for her rank.

She took off the cape she had been wearing and removed her bonnet.

She was washing her hands and was just about to dry them when there was a knock on the door.

When she said 'Come in' the Housekeeper appeared.

She was elderly and Kasia knew very like the Housekeeper who looked after their own house in the country.

"Good Afternoon, Miss Watson!" Mrs. Meadows said. "I'm sorry I wasn't here to welcome you, but you were early!"

She made it sound like a rebuke.

"We had a good journey down from London," Kasia said, "and I know that you are Mrs. Meadows."

She put out her hand and the Housekeeper shook it.

Kasia was aware once again that she looked too smart and too young to be a Governess.

"Your luncheon's just coming upstairs," Mrs. Meadows was saying, "and as soon as you've finished, I'll take you to meet Master Simon, if he hasn't disappeared in the meantime."

She spoke with a sharp note in her voice and Kasia asked:

"Is he in the habit of disappearing?"

"You never know what he'll get up to next!" Mrs. Meadows said. "I've tried leaving a housemaid with him, but he always manages to evade them if he has a mind to. Then there's a hue and cry until we find him again."

Kasia made no comment.

She was going into the Sitting-Room as she and Mrs. Meadows were talking.

The meal had been carried up on a tray by a footman, who placed on the table the first course.

"I'll come back as soon as you've finished," Mrs. Meadows said.

She moved towards the door.

"I think," Kasia replied, "I passed the School-Room which is just on the right as I was coming up the stairs."

"That's right," Mrs. Meadows answered.

"Then I think, if you do not mind," Kasia said, "I would like to go in unannounced. It might give me a better chance than if my pupil thinks I am yet another teacher."

"As you wish," Mrs. Meadows agreed. "In any case, I expect somebody has mentioned your arrival so Master Simon'll be expecting you."

Kasia hoped it was with something not so unpleasant as an ink-pot that he would greet her, but she did not say so.

She merely helped herself to the dishes that were being offered to her.

After watching her with an expression of surprise on her face, Mrs. Meadows left the room.

Because Kasia was hungry and the luncheon was well cooked, she ate a hearty meal.

She then drank a cup of coffee and told herself a little nervously that she was ready for the fray.

She waited until the footman had taken her tray

61

downstairs, then walked along the passage towards the School-Room.

As she opened the door she was aware there were footsteps on the other side of it.

She was not surprised as she went in to see a small boy at the far end of the room staring out of the window.

He had his back to her.

As she shut the door he said:

"If you are another Governess coming to teach me, you can go away!"

He spoke in a hard, aggressive tone and Kasia stood still, just inside the door.

Then she said in a low voice:

"Please . . please . . help . . me."

The young boy made no response and she moved forward saying very quietly:

"I want your help and, if you will listen, I will tell you . . why."

She got to within a few feet of him, then went no further.

After what seemed a long pause, the boy turned his head and looked at her.

"Why do you want me to help you?" he asked.

"It is a secret," Kasia replied.

He stared at her and she added, almost in a whisper:

"Look and see if there if anyone listening outside the door."

For a moment she feared he would refuse.

Then, as if his curiosity got the better of him, he pulled open the door.

He looked to left and right, then shut it again.

"There is nobody there."

"Good!" Kasia answered. "Now I can tell you without being overheard."

He came back towards her.

She saw that he was in fact a very attractive little boy, with dark brown hair and a clear expression.

He was dressed neatly in expensive clothes, but his shoe-laces were untied.

She guessed that he had refused to let anyone tie them for him.

She sat down on the sofa in front of the window.

Simon leaned against the end of it saying:

"You asked me to help you. What can I do?"

"If I do tell you," Kasia said, "will you 'cross your heart' and promise you will not tell anyone else?"

"What does 'cross your heart' mean?" Simon asked.

"It means that if you break your promise something awful will happen to you."

"What sort of thing? Will somebody shoot me, or hit me?"

"You might fall out of a window," Kasia said, "or drown in the lake."

"I will 'cross my heart'," he decided.

"You do it like this," Kasia explained.

She crossed her own heart and he copied her.

"Now, everything I am going to tell you is very, very secret," Kasia said in a whisper, "because if you tell I will be sent away."

"Why would you be sent away?" Simon asked.

"Because," Kasia said slowly, "I am not a real Governess. I am only pretending to be one."

Simon was obviously intrigued.

"Why should you pretend to be a Governess?" he asked.

Kasia looked round as if she was afraid someone was hiding in the corner.

Then she said in an even lower voice:

"I am in . . hiding!"

Simon sat down next to her.

"Who are you in hiding from?"

"Someone who is trying to make me do something I do not want to do, something horrible and wicked!"

"And so you have come here to hide!" Simon said.

Kasia nodded.

"That is right. I am hiding here in the castle, and no one will know how to find me."

She paused and looked at him before she added:

"That is . . if you will . . let me . . stay."

"You can stay, if you do not teach me," Simon said. "I hate people who teach!"

"I cannot teach you if I am only a pretend Governess," Kasia said. "At the same time, you will have to help me pretend . . otherwise the people here will say I am no good, and you must have . . somebody else."

Simon considered this for a moment.

Then he said:

"If we pretend to be doing lessons, they will not guess that you are not teaching me anything."

"That is right," Kasia said, "but we have to

64

pretend very cleverly so that they do not think for a moment that I am an imposter."

"I will help you," Simon said firmly.

"Oh .. thank you .. thank you!" Kasia cried. "It is very important I should hide here for the time being. But if you make them send me away, I shall have to do something very horrible which will make me desperately unhappy."

"They will not send you away if I say I want you to stay," Simon said.

"That is all I want," Kasia said, "but you must understand that we have to be very clever, so that they are completely deceived."

"How do we deceive them?" Simon enquired.

Kasia thought for a moment. Then she said:

"I think, as I have only just arrived, I would like to explore the garden while it is so sunny, and perhaps later on, or tomorrow, I could explore the Castle."

"I will show you in the garden," Simon offered.

"Then let us go now," Kasia suggested. "It looked very pretty as I came up the drive."

"You could not have seen the garden at the back," Simon said, "so I will take you there first."

"That is very kind of you," Kasia said, "and I am so grateful to you for saying you will help me."

"I will make sure that no one sends you away," Simon said, sounding quite grown-up.

"As I have already said, we shall have to be very clever about it," Kasia said in a conspiratorial voice.

"We will be," Simon answered. "Let us go into the garden before anyone tries to stop us."

He took Kasia down a staircase and out into the garden through a side-door where there was no one to see them.

The garden was, as Kasia had expected, very beautiful.

It was attractively laid out, and the yew hedges must have been growing there for centuries.

Simon took her over the lawns past a Bowling-Green.

Then they walked up a path which twisted and turned between the trees which sheltered the Castle from behind.

Many of the trees were very old. As they came to a great oak, Kasia said:

"That would be a good tree in which to hide!"

"I am not allowed to climb trees," Simon said.

"But I am!" Kasia replied. "And, if we hide among the branches no one will find us."

"I have always wanted to climb a tree," Simon said a little doubtfully, "but no one would let me try. They said I might fall and hurt myself."

"Of course you will do nothing so silly!" Kasia said. "I will show you how to climb a tree, but first we must take off our shoes."

She took off her shoes, then Simon did the same.

Regardless of her pretty gown, Kasia began to pull herself up by a low branch.

Simon watched her and then tackled another.

Kasia had carefully chosen an easy tree to climb, but she had in fact been climbing trees all her life.

66

Her Mother had encouraged her to do so.

"I always used to climb a tree if I wanted to hide from my Governess," Lady Margaret had said. "It used to amuse me to hear her calling me, while I was just above her hiding among the leaves."

She had paused before she continued:

"But I was frequently punished for the mess I made of my clothes."

There had been a special tree in the garden of her home where Kasia liked to sit and think.

It had a beautiful view of the surrounding country.

She used to feel as if she was looking down from Heaven at the people striving below.

"I am sure the angels when they are looking at us," she told herself, "often think how silly we are to keep looking down at the earth instead of up at the stars."

Without her helping him Simon reached her.

She thought that one reason why he was so difficult was that he had never been allowed to extend himself physically.

'This is really his first lesson,' she thought, 'and, in my opinion, a very sensible one!'

Simon sat down beside her with his legs dangling over a thick oak bough.

"I have done it!" he exclaimed excitedly. "I have done it!"

"Of course you have!" Kasia smiled. "Now we are so high that no one can find us."

The oak leaves were very thick.

She parted them a little so that she could look back at the garden and over the lake which lay below the house.

There was a Park beyond in which she was sure she could see speckled deer.

Then Simon said:

"There is someone coming!"

He was right.

A man was walking between the yew hedges and over the Bowling-Green.

"Keep very still," Kasia whispered, "and he will not know we are here."

She let go of the leaves she was holding so that they obscured them once again from view.

. . . .

The Duke had arrived in under two hours, and on reaching the Castle, had immediately set to work.

He had sent for the Estate Manager and told him he wished to inspect the Home Farm.

He also would hear what the Farmers required to bring their flocks and their crops up to date.

The Estate Manager said he would make arrangements for the Duke to visit at least four farms the following day.

He suggested that they started after an early breakfast.

The Duke agreed.

He was aware that the Estate Manager wished to give the Farmers a chance to 'tidy up' and look their best.

He then saw Mr. Bennett and told him that he wanted to see the Estate painters, carpenters and stonemasons.

There was a great deal to be done to the Castle itself.

"They will have to come tomorrow afternoon, Your Grace," Mr. Bennett said. "They are all at work and it would take too long to collect them now."

Again the Duke agreed.

At the same time he thought he now had more or less a free afternoon when he had in fact expected to be busy.

He wanted to see what new horses had already arrived in the stables.

He intended to inform his Head Groom there were more arriving either today or tomorrow.

He had purchased a number at Tattersall's Sale-Rooms and left bids for others.

Mr. Ashton had told him before he left London that they were accepted.

Now it was just a question of their being delivered, which had been arranged by his grooms in Berkeley Square.

Mr. Bennett had made a list of some of the work which had to be done in the Castle.

The Duke when he had finished his luncheon, read the list before he walked out into the garden.

As he did so, he thought he had been a fool to spend so long in London when the country was enchanting.

Nothing could be more peaceful.

It was only as he was walking across the lawn that he remembered that he had forgotten about his little nephew Simon and how tiresome he was.

While he had been dancing attendance on Lady Julie, the Castle and its difficulties had seemed far away.

Now he felt rather guilty.

He had been fond of his brother and extremely upset when he had been killed.

After the War ended, he had spent two years with the Army of Occupation in France.

It was not until he had returned to England that he learnt his brother's only child had caused such difficulties among his relatives.

Charles's wife had died a year after he had been killed.

The small boy had been taken from their home which was put up for sale by the Trustees.

He and his Nanny had then stayed first with one of his Mother's sisters.

She however soon said that two extra people in the house was too much for her.

Simon had then been sent to one of the Horne relatives.

She was an elderly Aunt, who soon found a small child an intolerable burden.

He had moved on and on.

The Duke learned that finally all the relatives approached by the Trustees refused to take responsibility for him.

Dreghorne Castle was the only place left.

The Duke had said in an airy way:

"There is room for a regiment of small boys, and there will certainly be no difficulty in having Simon!"

He had not been aware then of the problem of Simon's education.

His brother had put him down for Eton almost as soon as he was born.

Both he and Darcy had been very happy there.

The Duke was soon to realise that neither Eton, nor any other School, would take Simon, if he remained as ignorant as he was at the moment.

He had instructed Mr. Bennett and Mr. Ashton to advertise first for a Governess, then for Tutors.

One after another they came, one after another they quickly went.

The Duke was anxious to do his best for his nephew.

But he really had not time to concentrate on a small boy when there were so many interesting things happening in London.

Especially with Beauties like Lady Julie to keep him amused.

But no boy, he thought, could fail to enjoy himself in any place so delightful as the Castle.

'And it is mine!' he was thinking. 'Mine for as long as I live, and what man could ask for more?'

He walked on, thinking of how the Castle had always fascinated him when he was young.

His Father and Mother had lived only about five miles away, and he had frequently gone with them to the Castle.

There they could play with their Cousins who were about the same age as they were.

They were rich and had everything they could possibly desire.

They were however only too willing to share everything including their horses with them.

He swam with them in the lake and raced them each trying to jump higher hedges than the other.

Never had he thought that one day the Castle might be his.

He walked on, going up a little path he remembered well.

It led to the top of the wood from which there was a magnificent view.

Then as he passed one of the large oak trees he saw something white on the ground beneath it.

He looked in surprise at an elegant pair of white slippers.

Then he saw that beside them lay a pair of boy's shoes.

CHAPTER FOUR

The Duke stood for a moment looking down at the shoes, then he raised his head.

The leaves were very thick.

But almost directly above him he saw two large eyes staring at him.

The leaves fell back and he walked forward.

He was against the truck of the tree when he looked up again.

Above him there was a very attractive young girl sitting on a thick bough.

She had a small, heart-shaped face, and her eyes, which he had seen through the leaves, were almost too big for it.

Then he was aware that his nephew was only a foot or so away from her.

"Hello, Simon," he said, "you seem to have moved up in the world! And who is your friend?"

Quickly, because Kasia thought Simon was looking sulky, Kasia said:

"I am the new Governess, Your Grace. My name is Watson."

The Duke stared at her as if he could not believe

his ears.

After a long pause while they just looked at each other he said:

"And are you telling me, Miss Watson, that this is a lesson?"

"Of course, Your Grace," Kasia replied. "It is the study of nature combined with gymnastic exercise."

The Duke gave a short laugh as if he could not help it.

Then he said:

"In which case I must not interfere, but I hope, after I have been to the stables, you will both have tea with me."

He turned as he spoke and went back the way he had come.

Only when he was out of ear-shot did Simon say:

"That was Uncle Darcy."

"I realise that," Kasia replied, "but I thought he could not be here because the flag was not flying over the Castle."

There was silence for a moment.

Then Simon said as if the words were dragged from him:

"I tore it and they are having it repaired."

"You tore it?" Kasia questioned. "How did you manage to do that?"

"I went up on the roof," Simon explained, "and Mr. Jackson was very angry. He started to drag me back, but I held onto the flag."

"So it tore!" Kasia said. "I expect it can be mended all right, or they can buy a new one."

"Mr. Jackson tried to punish me," Simon went on, "by making me write out twenty times 'I must not go on the roof'."

"And did you do that?" Kasia enquired.

"I threw an ink-pot at him," Simon said with a note of relish in his voice.

Kasia laughed.

"I heard about that. I hope you will not throw one at me!"

"No, of course not," Simon said, "and you would not make me write out such silly things."

"You may have to pretend to write," Kasia said after a little pause, "because your Uncle will ask what you are learning."

Simon thought this over.

But before he could say anything, Kasia said:

"Let us go to the top of the wood, until your Uncle has left the stables. I want to look at the horses. Do you ride?"

"I hate riding!" Simon answered.

"You hate it?" Kasia repeated. "How can you hate it? I think it is the most exciting thing anyone can do."

"They make me ride a horrid little pony," Simon said, "and the groom keeps me on a leading-rein."

"That is the silliest thing I have ever heard!" Kasia exclaimed. "Of course you are too old to be on a leading-rein, and you want a horse – a big one!"

"They will not let me have one," Simon grumbled.

"They will, if I insist upon it," Kasia said, "and I would love to ride with you. Oh, please, Simon, let us try to ride together. It will be such fun!"

"And I can have a horse?" Simon asked.

"I am sure I can arrange for you to have what you want," Kasia said.

She was thinking it would be easier if they went to the stables and simply ordered horses.

"I tell you what we will do," she said. "We will say nothing now, but tomorrow morning early, perhaps before your Uncle is up, we will go to the stables and choose the horses we want to ride."

She smiled at him before continuing:

"Then if you do not fall off, but enjoy it, they will not be able to forbid you to do it again."

"That sounds a spiffing idea!" Simon said.

Kasia guessed that he had got the adjective from one of the footmen, but she merely smiled.

"Now I am going to get down," she said. "You can follow me, but let me go first."

She swung herself lithely down from the bough, hung by her hands and then dropped the last few feet.

The ground was soft and covered with moss.

She knew if he fell Simon would not be hurt, and told him what to do.

He obeyed her, but landed a little awkwardly on his knees.

He did not hurt himself and said as he picked himself up:

"That was fun!"

"I was sure you would think so," Kasia said, "and we will soon climb much higher trees, where no one will be able to find us."

"Yes, let us do that," Simon agreed.

They walked up to the top of the wood as the Duke had intended to do.

As Kasia saw the view spread out before her towards an indefinite horizon she drew in her breath.

To her it was so lovely that she felt as if she was seeing the world from a different angle than she had ever seen it before.

Then, as if she came back to earth again, she remembered that Simon was with her.

"Now you have shown me this beautiful view," she said, "where shall we go next?"

"Let us go to the stables," Simon suggested. "I am sure Uncle Darcy will not stay there long."

"Why do you think that?" Kasia asked.

"They keep saying how much work he has to do now he is the Duke," Simon said.

Kasia thought this showed that Simon was in fact, interested in what went on around him.

As they walked through the wood she said:

"I have always loved the woods. When I was little I used to listen to the trees where I believed the goblins were working underneath them. We had a pool at home which I was sure was full of water-nymphs."

"Nanny used to tell me stories about goblins and fairies," Simon said.

"And where is your Nanny now?" Kasia asked.

"They sent her away. Aunt Martha said I was too old to have a Nanny, but Nanny said it was because she was so mean that she grudged her the food she put in her mouth."

"I am sure you miss her," Kasia said sympathetically.

"I ran away to try to find her," Simon said, "but they brought me back and were very angry."

Kasia thought it was shocking that he had been treated in a way which would upset any sensitive child.

She did not say anything however.

Instead she told Simon a story about the way the Ancient Britons used to ambush the invading Roman Army in the woods.

She finished the story just before the stables came in sight.

Then she drew up behind some bushes and said:

"Let us peep to make sure your Uncle is not still there."

Simon was delighted to do this.

They crept through the bushes until they could see clearly that the stable-yard was empty.

One of the lads came out of a stable-door carrying a pail and he was whistling.

Kasia thought he was not likely to be doing that if the Duke was anywhere near.

She and Simon therefore went into the yard.

She quickly asked that he himself should show her the horses, although after they had been there a short while a grown man appeared.

Kasia held out her hand.

"I must introduce myself," she said. "I am Miss Watson, the new Governess, and I want my pupil, Master Simon, to show me the horses."

"We've some fine noo uns," the man replied,

who she was to learn later was the Head Groom.

"I felt sure you would have," Kasia said, "and as I love horses, I very much want to see them."

Simon had gone into one of the stalls.

"Come and see this horse, Miss Watson," he shouted.

As she moved towards him the Head Groom said:

"That be one us 'ave 'ad fer sometime, an' a very nice animal it be."

Inside the stall Simon was patting a mare which Kasia could see was well bred.

The animal was obviously pleased with the boy's attention.

Kasia made a note that that was the one she would ask to be saddled for him in the morning.

She did not however say anything about riding.

She just went from stall to stall, finding the new animals that had arrived from London were some of the finest horse-flesh she had ever seen.

Simon however, kept going back to the mare, who was called '*Princess*.'

"She likes me!" he said excitedly.

Kasia thought he was thrilled that the horse liked him simply because no one else had shown him any love.

However, time was getting on, and knowing it would be a mistake for Simon to be late for tea with his Uncle, Kasia insisted they must return to the Castle.

"I will come back and see *Princess* tomorrow," Simon said when they were alone.

"And, if you like, ride her," Kasia said.

Simon's eyes lit up.

"Can I do that?"

"I am sure you can, but do not talk about it just in case anyone says no."

"They are sure to say that," Simon complained. "Everybody says no to everything I want to do."

"Well, you said yes to me, when I asked you to help me to hide," Kasia replied. "So be careful to behave nicely at tea, otherwise they might send me away."

"I will not let Uncle Darcy send you away!" Simon said fiercely.

"I want to stay," Kasia said, "so, Simon, please be very polite, and let him think you are going to work hard at your lessons."

She thought Simon was going to protest at the word 'lessons', and she added:

"Your Uncle and Mr. Bennett and everybody else thinks I am too young to be your Governess, so we have to be clever and persuade them that I am teaching you lots of things you ought to know."

Simon nodded his head and she thought he understood.

They went upstairs to the School-Room and she persuaded him to change into a different suit.

There was a maid to help him change, and she went into her own room.

There were dirty marks on her gown where she had climbed the tree.

She quickly changed into a fresh one which she knew was far too expensive for a Governess.

But it was the simplest of those she had brought with her.

She and Simon went downstairs to find the Duke in an attractive room which overlooked the rose-garden at the back of the Castle.

The furniture was mostly French.

Kasia saw at once that there were several beautiful pictures by French artists on the walls.

The Duke was reading the newspaper when they appeared.

He put it down and rose to his feet to say:

"Tea has just arrived, so you are commendably punctual after your walk."

"We went to the top of the hill, Your Grace," Kasia said, "from which there is the most wonderful view I have ever seen!"

"It is what I have always enjoyed myself," the Duke said, "and what do you think it taught Simon?"

She thought he was testing her and she answered simply:

"I think it made him feel that he was looking down from Heaven on human beings, and that we should all, in some way, try to guide and help them."

The Duke looked at her in astonishment.

Then he said:

"Will you pour out, Miss Watson?"

There was an impressive silver tea-pot, kettle, cream-jug, and sugar-basin on the table in front of a sofa.

Kasia sat down to pour out the tea into the china cups.

As she did so, she said without thinking:

"We have the same Chamberlain Worcester service at home, and every time I see it, I think how pretty it is."

Only after she had spoken, and because the silence was embarrassing, did she remember that a Governess was not likely to own such expensive china.

The Duke said nothing, but accepted the cup and saucer she handed to him.

Kasia turned to Simon.

"Do you like tea, Simon?" she asked, "or would you prefer milk, or perhaps lemonade?"

"They will not give me lemonade," Simon said, "because there are no lemons, so they said."

The Duke laughed.

"I expect, if that happened yesterday, they will have some by now."

He pulled the bell and when the door opened he said:

"Master Simon would like some lemonade instead of tea. Please see it is available for him in the future."

"Very good, Your Grace," the Butler replied.

"That is very kind of you," Kasia said.

She looked at Simon as she spoke and made a little movement with her eyes.

He understood and said:

"Thank you, Uncle Darcy. I like lemonade."

"I liked it too when I was your age," the Duke said, "and I would certainly have enjoyed it if I had been able to have it during the war."

"Oh, do tell us about the war," Kasia begged. "I know you did great deeds and won lots of medals, but I am sure no one has told Simon about it."

The Duke looked surprised.

He would have thought it an ordinary topic of conversation in the Castle, if nowhere else.

"They would not talk to me about the war," Simon said, "because when I was staying with Cousin Amy I said I was going to be like Uncle Darcy and shoot everyone who was an enemy."

The Duke laughed.

"I am not surprised you frightened them."

"I was trying to be like you," Simon said.

"I will tell you some stories about the war," the Duke answered, "but just now I have to cope with the peace, and that means there are a lot of things to be done here in the Castle and outside."

"I am sure Simon would like to help you," Kasia said.

She realised as she spoke that it was an idea that had never occurred to the Duke.

He wondered quickly what the child could do.

"Of course," he said aloud, "I shall want all the help I can get. In fact, it would be a good idea if Simon and you, Miss Watson, wrote me a list of everything that you see in the house that wants repairing, painting or attending to in some way. Then you can add what you find outside in the grounds."

Kasia realised he was inviting his nephew, who had refused to have any lessons, to write.

"That is an excellent idea," she said. "Simon and I will have a competition to see who can have the most items on our list."

The Duke's eyes twinkled.

"In which case," he said, "I suppose you will expect me to provide a prize at the end."

"But of course!" Kasia answered. "It would be no fun without one!"

She saw that Simon was thinking it over.

Because she was afraid he might refuse to do anything which involved him in writing, she said:

"This is a very beautiful room, Your Grace, and I am thrilled to see that you have a Boucher amongst your collection of pictures."

"I was thrilled myself when I first saw it," the Duke said, "but as I am sure you are aware, it needs cleaning, and the same applies to nearly all the paintings in the Picture Gallery."

"That is a place I especially want to see, Simon," Kasia said turning towards the little boy.

She felt he should not be left out of the conversation and Simon replied:

"You said you would explore the garden first."

"Yes, I know," Kasia said, "but there is so much to explore, and for me it is very, very exciting."

The Duke talked a little more about the pictures.

Kasia was amused at his surprise that she knew so much about the artists.

She was well aware that he was looking at her contemplatively as if he was not quite sure that she was genuine.

He suspected that someone so young and well-dressed coming to the Castle as a Governess must be some sort of joke.

As soon as Simon had finished his tea, and had

said very little while he was eating, Kasia rose to her feet.

"I think, Your Grace, Simon and I should leave you as I am sure you have so much to do. And as I have only just arrived, I have to find my way about and have a lot to learn about how things are managed here."

"I am sure, Miss Watson, you will soon have them managed to your satisfaction," the Duke said with just a touch of mockery in his voice.

Kasia was aware that Simon was already walking towards the door.

As she was about to follow him the Duke said:

"I would like to talk to you, Miss Watson, about my nephew's education."

He paused for a moment, wondering whether it would be possible to ask her to dine with him.

Then he knew that the household would think it very strange.

He was thinking back to when he was Simon's age and younger.

He remembered that the Governess or Tutor who taught him came down to luncheon.

But she always had dinner in their own quarters.

It was one of the unwritten laws which he was sure was still adhered to.

Miss Watson was certainly a very unusual Governess, and quite obviously a Lady.

Yet it would be a mistake for her to be gossiped about below stairs.

"I think the best time," he said in a somewhat lofty manner, "would be after dinner. As I shall be dining alone, I should be free at about a quarter to nine so will you join me either here, or in the Library?"

"Yes, of course, Your Grace," Kasia said in a subservient tone.

She curtsied, then followed Simon to the door.

She was well aware as she did so that the Duke was watching her, and, she thought, suspiciously.

Simon ran up the stairs, and she followed him.

When they reached the School-Room, he said:

"I was good, Miss Watson! I did not do anything bad!"

"You were very, very good, and it was a splendid piece of acting," Kasia said.

"Why do you think Uncle Darcy wants to see you after dinner?" Simon enquired.

Kasia sat down in one of the armchairs.

"I am sure he is going to give me a long list of all the things I have to teach you," she answered. "History, Geography, Arithmetic, and lots more!"

Simon gave a shout.

"I will not – I will not do it! I will not learn!"

"I am only teasing," Kasia said. "And do not worry. Whatever your Uncle suggests, I will agree to, and I will just pretend to do what he wants."

"That is a spiffing idea!" Simon said. "I was afraid you might be frightened of him and carry out his orders."

"I am not a soldier," Kasia replied, "so I do not have to. In fact you, and only you, know I am a fugitive, hiding in the Castle so that no one will find me."

"You do not think Uncle Darcy will suspect you are not what you pretend to be?" Simon asked.

Kasia thought this was indeed very likely, but it would be a mistake to let Simon think so.

"We must be very careful and act cleverly, so that he believes I am just a Governess from whom you are learning lots and lots of things, which he believes are important."

"He may be very angry when he finds out we have been deceiving him," Simon said.

"Then we must be careful that he does not find out!" Kasia said. "And if the people from whom I am hiding are looking for me, they must never think that the Governess at the Castle is the person they have lost."

"We must deceive them too," Simon said.

There was a note of excitement in his voice.

Kasia knew he was finding all this pretence and acting unexpectedly thrilling.

"You have been very clever up to date," she said, "and I am sure your Uncle did not expect you to behave so well at tea, or be so polite, and that is what you must go on being to everybody!"

"And that will make them think you are a very good Governess," Simon said.

"Of course it will," Kasia replied.

She walked to the table on which she saw had been left a number of pencils and a few sheets of paper, besides exercise-books.

"You must not forget," she said, "that we have to make the lists for your Uncle."

She thought Simon was going to refuse to do it and she said quickly:

"I wonder what he will give us as a prize? What would you like to have if he asked you?"

Simon thought for a moment before he said:

"I would like some money."

"Money?" Kasia questioned in astonishment. "Why money?"

"Because they never let me have any."

"Do you mean you do not have any pocket-money?" she asked.

Simon shook his head.

"I had some when I was staying with one Aunt, but she was angry because I tried to go to the shops to buy some sweeties."

"You mean you tried to go alone?" Kasia asked.

"They were old and said they were too tired to walk to the village," Simon explained.

"And you have never had any pocket-money since then?"

"It is no use my having any pocket-money if I have nowhere to spend it," Simon replied logically.

"Well, prize or no prize," Kasia said, "I will ask for you to have some pocket-money every week, and then you and I will go shopping. You shall buy what you want, and I am sure there are lots of things I forgot to pack into my trunk."

"That would be fun!" Simon said. "I would like that very much!"

"Then that is what we will do," Kasia said, "and we might even buy a present for your Uncle. That would surprise him!"

"I want to buy some sweeties," Simon said.

"Of course you do, and I used to buy them every week with my pocket-money," Kasia said, "but I also saved up and bought presents for my Father and Mother at Christmas, and they were very pleased with what I gave them."

There was a little pause. Then Simon said:

"When I have some pocket-money I will buy you a present!"

Kasia clasped her hands together.

"Oh, Simon, how kind of you! I would love a present, I really would! But it must be a surprise, so you must not tell me what it is before you give it to me."

Simon looked pleased and after a moment she said:

"Do not forget that we are going to win a prize from your Uncle, and that too will be a surprise."

"I do not want to write, and I said I would not write!" Simon said as if he had just remembered.

"That is what you said to Mr. Jackson, who was obviously a silly man," Kasia said. "But you and I will be writing things which will help your Uncle and make the Castle even more exciting than it is at the moment."

She put her fingers up to her face as she said:

"I have just been thinking that you are a very lucky boy to live in such an exciting, thrilling place."

She paused a moment before she went on:

"I will tell you a story tomorrow about a Castle nearly as big as this one, where they fought against the Vikings when they came in their big ships across the North Sea to steal cows, sheep and women."

"What happened?" Simon asked.

"The people in the Castle were so brave and fought so gallantly that the Vikings went away without any of the booty they had expected to steal."

She saw that Simon was listening, and said:

"That is what you have to do here, and make your Castle so strong that if anyone attacked you, you would be able to drive them away."

"Can I have a gun?" Simon asked.

"Of course if you are fighting you will want a gun! But you would have to learn how to use it first."

Simon thought about this and after a moment Kasia said:

"I can see what your Uncle means when he says there is a lot to be done. There are bricks that need pointing at the front of the Castle, and I expect the reason why they did not want you to go up on the roof is that it needs repairing."

Simon had obviously never thought of that and now he said:

"Shall we put that down on the list?"

"I think we ought to," Kasia said, "and tomorrow we will look everywhere we go to find things that need doing."

"I want to start now," Simon said.

"Very well," Kasia agreed, "bring a pencil and a piece of paper and we will do this corridor first, and all the windows on it, then gradually work down, day by day, to the front of the Castle."

She glanced at the clock and said:

"If we do that for half-an-hour, that will give me time to tell you a very exciting story about the invasion of England by William of Normandy before you go to bed."

"I would like that, I would like it very much," Simon said.

As he spoke he picked up a pencil from the table and took one of the sheets of paper.

"I think it would be easier to write it down in an exercise-book," Kasia suggested. "We must put an 'S' against the things you find, and a 'K' against mine."

" 'K'?" Simon queried.

"That is for my Christian name, which is Kasia," she answered.

She spoke without thinking, then put her fingers up to her mouth.

"Oh!" she exclaimed. "I had forgotten, and that is another secret."

"What is?" Simon asked.

"My name. I told Mr. Bennett that my Christian name was 'Kate', but actually it is 'Kasia'!"

"I like that! It is much prettier than Kate!" Simon said.

"That was what I thought, but you must not tell anyone, and I only told you by mistake."

"I will tell no one," Simon said. " 'Cross my heart'!"

CHAPTER FIVE

After dinner Kasia went downstairs.

She was wearing what was one of the prettiest of her evening-gowns.

It was beautiful but, she was well aware, far too elaborate for a Governess.

When she walked into the Drawing-Room the Duke was standing in front of the fireplace, obviously waiting for her.

He watched her as she moved towards him.

He was thinking that she was exceedingly graceful, as well as, he admitted to himself, very lovely.

"Good evening, Miss Watson," he said, "if that is your real name. Will you sit down?"

Kasia looked at him, but she did not speak and he went on:

"Now I think we should 'get down to brass tacks'. Why are you here? Is it blackmail? Or perhaps just a flattering desire to meet me?"

Kasia looked up at him in sheer astonishment.

Then she said slowly:

"I cannot imagine why you should think it is for either of those reasons."

"You must give me credit for having some intelligence," the Duke replied. "Why should anyone as beautiful as you, dressed extremely expensively, want to be a Governess to a boy who is completely out of hand, unless the reason is that he is my nephew?"

Kasia realised that, although he was speaking pleasantly, he was insulting her.

"You are very mistaken, Your Grace," she said, "if you think I came to the Castle because I wanted to meet you."

She stopped speaking for a moment, then continued:

"When I answered the advertisement which your Secretary had put in the *Morning Post* I had no idea that you were in any way connected with the boy who needed a Governess."

"In that case of course I apologise for the second suggestion. But the first remains."

Kasia could not help thinking it was rather funny, seeing how rich she was, but she simply said:

"I can assure Your Grace that I have no intention of blackmailing anyone."

"Then we get back to the basic question: why are you here?"

There was a pause, then Kasia said:

"I think, without meaning to be rude, that that is my business."

"It is also mine," the Duke retorted, "as you are in my employment to look after my nephew."

As she did not answer he said:

"You came from London and you were therefore

interviewed by Mr. Ashton. Surely he took your references?"

Kasia was aware that this was a weak point in her case, and she said after a moment:

"I offered him one, but it would have taken time for him to take it up, and I wished to be in the appointment immediately."

"Why?" the Duke asked.

"I had to leave the place where I was staying."

"Did they dismiss you, or did you leave of your own free will?" the Duke asked.

"Of my own free will," Kasia replied.

There was silence. Then he said:

"I do not seem to be getting any further in this."

"Why should you want to?" Kasia asked. "You can see for yourself that Simon has accepted me, and may I say, Your Grace, that I think he has been very badly treated and is still neglected in a way I find incredible!"

"Neglected!" the Duke exclaimed.

He was obviously, she saw, genuinely surprised at what she had just said.

"Of course I have only just arrived," Kasia said, "but from what I have heard, he has been pushed 'from pillar to post', unloved and not considered as a living, breathing human being by anyone who has looked after him."

The Duke stared at her.

"You astound me, Miss Watson," he said. "I cannot believe that this has been happening here."

"Well it has," Kasia answered, "and I am more

sorry for Simon than I can possibly express in words."

She thought the Duke did not believe her and she said:

"Did you know that everything he has asked for has been denied him? He has not been allowed to ride, except on a small pony led by a groom, and the way he is fed is quite appalling."

"What do you mean by that?" the Duke demanded.

"I discovered this evening that he was given for his supper bread and milk, and a rather nasty spoonful of pudding. Had you not ordered lemonade for him, he would have had water."

"I cannot believe it!" the Duke said. "Surely he could have asked for what he wanted?"

"Judging from the way he has been refused everything else that has interested him, I am quite certain no notice would have been taken. He, however, enjoyed my supper which I shared with him."

The Duke sat down on a chair before he said:

"Are you really prepared, looking as you do, to stay here in the Castle and turn Simon from what I have been told is a monster into a decent human being?"

"That is what he is, with me," Kasia said.

The Duke looked at her, then he said:

"Then I can only apologise for what I have been saying, and ask you to continue to look after my nephew and make him, as I have just said, into a human being who will, I hope, be able to go to Eton."

Kasia did not reply and after a moment he went on:

"You must be aware that I am consumed with curiosity. I find it extremely frustrating not to know why you are here, and also why you are so different from anyone else I have ever met."

Kasia smiled.

"I hope that is true, Your Grace, and if you will trust me to do what I want to do with Simon, I feel sure that he will soon be very different from what he has been in the past."

"I simply cannot believe all this!" the Duke said. "You cannot look like you do, appear very young, and yet be so wise and intelligent."

Kasia laughed.

"That is the nicest compliment I have ever had! Thank you!"

"That is another thing I find it impossible to believe," the Duke said. "If you have been in London you must have been overwhelmed with compliments."

She did not say anything, and he looked at her for a long moment before he went on:

"Where did you get that gown?"

Because it was a question she had not expected at that moment, she replied after a little pause:

"It was a . . present from a . . friend."

"That is what I rather suspected," the Duke said.

She did not understand the sarcastic note in his voice and after a moment she said:

"I know that you are in a position, Your Grace, where you are entitled to ask me questions, and I would answer them if I could. But I am asking you to let me keep my secrets to myself for as long as is necessary."

"So you admit to having secrets!" the Duke took her up quickly. "Now that you have said that, I suspect you are hiding from something or somebody."

She thought he was being cleverer than she expected and she held up her hands.

"Please . . please," she begged, "everything is for the moment . . going well. Do not . . spoil . . it."

As she spoke she thought she might be speaking to Simon.

"Very well, Miss Watson, you win!" the Duke conceded. "We will just have to wait and see what happens."

Kasia smiled at him.

"Thank you," she said. "Now instead of talking about me, which I find very boring, could we please talk about you. There are so many things I want to know."

. . . .

Looking back later at their conversation the Duke thought it was very different from any conversation he had ever had with a beautiful woman.

Kasia had said she wanted to talk about him.

But it was not about him as a man!

It was about the battles in which he had fought, the situation in France with the Army of Occupation, and his impression so far of the peace.

The Duke thought he might have been talking with one of his male contemporaries.

When he remembered what had been said, he was aware that the questions Kasia had put to him were extremely intelligent.

Never once had she looked at him with that inevitable invitation in her eyes.

Never had there been an unspoken desire for him on her lips.

In fact as far as he was concerned the whole evening might have been a part of his imagination and not real.

. . . .

Kasia awoke very early.

Having dressed herself in her riding-habit, she went through the School-Room into the bedroom occupied by Simon.

She woke him up.

Ten minutes later they slipped down the back stairs and went towards the stables.

It was so early that only the two grooms who were on night-duty were there.

Without any comment they bridled and saddled the horses Kasia chose.

Simon was mounted first on *Princess*.

Kasia was aware that he was thrilled and excited at being allowed to ride a horse.

She longed to choose for herself one of the new arrivals which had come from Tattersall's.

They were very spirited.

But she thought that might upset *Princess*.

Instead she chose a well bred older horse which she guessed had been in the stables before the Duke came into the title.

Because she did not wish them to be seen by anyone at the Castle they left the stable-yard by the back entrance.

It took them as Kasia hoped, into the paddocks.

She trotted onto the smooth ground, encouraging Simon to ride quite fast.

She saw with relief that he seemed instinctively to know how to handle a horse.

She was quite certain that the Duke was a good rider.

Therefore his brother, Simon's Father, would also have been good.

By the time they had ridden all round the paddock she was satisfied that Simon was confident enough to go further afield.

They rode off along some level ground which had a stream running through it.

Only when they were quite a long way from the Castle did Simon say:

"I can ride! You see? I can *ride*, Miss Watson! Now no one can stop me from riding a big horse like *Princess*."

"Of course not," Kasia said, "and I am sure your Uncle will be delighted."

She was not surprised when they turned for home to see in the distance the Duke coming towards them.

She felt sure that he would ride before breakfast,

just as her Father always did when they were in the country.

He would have been told in the stables that she and Simon had already gone out.

"There is your Uncle, Simon," she said. "Now go towards him, so that he can see how well you ride."

Simon set off and she deliberately hung back.

This was the moment when the Duke must think only of his nephew and be impressed by him.

She was not mistaken, for as she rode up a few minutes later, it was to hear the Duke saying:

"That was very good, Simon. Your Father, if he were here, would be very proud of you."

"Miss Watson says I am too old to ride a pony, and be led about," Simon said.

"And she is of course quite right," the Duke answered.

He looked at Kasia as he spoke and his eyes were twinkling.

"I have learned that lesson," he said, "and I will not make the same mistake again."

She laughed.

"It was not entirely your fault, and there are an awful lot of stupid people in the world."

"If you are counting me amongst them," the Duke said, "I shall be extremely annoyed!"

"I do not think anyone could say that you were stupid," Kasia replied, "but perhaps just rather ignorant about young boys."

"I was one myself once."

"And I expect you were very adventurous and continually in trouble!" Kasia retorted.

The Duke laughed.

Then he told himself that the most extraordinary thing about this young Governess was that she was not in awe of him.

In fact, she behaved as if she was his equal.

He had been watching the way she rode and decided she was used to riding well-bred, expensive horses.

"Why did she come here?" he asked himself for the thousandth time.

They did not see any more of the Duke that morning.

Kasia was informed that she and Simon were expected to have luncheon in the Dining-Room.

That was, she knew, correct.

Simon said he would rather have luncheon alone with her, but she made him brush his hair and wash his hands before they joined the Duke.

"Be careful what you say you have done this morning," she warned him as they went downstairs. "We should have been doing lessons."

She thought with a smile that was exactly what they had been doing!

But definitely not the sort that appeared in any School curriculum.

She and Simon had gone to see the Picture Gallery.

They made notes there about a large number of the pictures which needed cleaning, and some which had damaged frames.

She told Simon interesting stories about some of the artists.

They had then gone into the Library.

Kasia had exclaimed in delight at the enormous number of books it held.

"I hate books and I do not want to read!" Simon said angrily.

"I do not want you to read anything," Kasia said, "but you remember that story I told you last night about William the Conqueror? I thought it might be fun to try to find a picture of him. After all, he was the first great King of all England."

She saw a look of interest on Simon's face and said:

"I will race you to see who finds a picture of him first, and the prize will be a four-penny piece."

Simon reacted to this.

With a little bit of pushing books in the right direction, she made him find King William the First.

Simon was delighted.

"That was clever of me, was it not, Miss Watson?" he asked.

"Very clever!" Kasia agreed, "and here is the four-penny piece. You can spend it with your other pocket-money, when we go shopping this afternoon."

She had seen Mr. Bennett immediately after breakfast.

He had agreed to give Simon sixpence pocket-money every week.

She had then ordered a pony-cart which she found to her surprise did exist in the stables.

"You can have a carriage, if you want one, Miss Watson," Mr. Bennett said.

"No, thank you, I would rather have the pony-cart," Kasia said. "I am sure Simon will want to drive back."

Mr. Bennett looked at her and smiled.

"They have come to the conclusion below stairs, Miss Watson, that you are a Witch!" he said. "We have never known Master Simon behave so well before!"

"If I am a Witch, then I hope I am a White one!" Kasia said. "I do not wish to end up being burnt at the stake!"

"I sincerely hope that will not happen!" Mr. Bennett replied.

Simon was delighted with his pocket-money, with which he could buy the sweeties he wanted.

When he had done so, Kasia deliberately bought a number of items for herself.

She asked Simon if he would jot them down on a little note-book she carried in her bag.

She chose several pieces of soap, a new tooth-brush, some hair-pins, and a few yards of pretty pink ribbon.

As the Shopkeeper wrapped it all up for her, she said to Simon:

"Please, Simon, will you add it all up for me?"

She gave him a warning look in case he should refuse in front of the Shopkeeper.

She was quite certain that everyone in the village had heard about Simon's behaviour with the Tutors.

Simon was astute enough to realise he must at

least pretend to add up the figures he had written down.

Actually he did it correctly.

Kasia thanked him.

As she picked up her parcels she said:

"Please will you open my bag, Simon? You will find some money in the purse."

Very carefully, Simon counted it out and the Shopkeeper took it, coin by coin.

When they got outside and were back in the pony-cart, Kasia said:

"That was very clever of you, and now it will go all round the village that you can do Arithmetic!"

"I thought that was what you wanted me to do," Simon said.

"You have been brilliant, and now I have a surprise for you!" Kasia said.

"A surprise?" Simon asked.

"I have found out from Mr. Bennett that only a month ago your Nanny was given a cottage at the end of the village!"

"Nanny!" Simon exclaimed.

"I thought you might like to call and see her."

"Of course I want to see Nanny!" Simon answered.

When Kasia had asked the question of Mr. Bennett, he had said:

"It is strange that you should ask that, Miss Watson. It was only three weeks ago that the old woman wrote to me saying she was desperate. I learned to my consternation that she received no pension after she had been dismissed by one of Master Simon's relatives."

"No pension?" Kasia questioned.

"It must have been an oversight," Mr. Bennett said in an apologetic voice, "but she has come to the end of her savings and, as you can understand, was afraid that she might have to go to the Workhouse."

"How could something like that happen to a Nanny, of all people?" Kasia asked.

"I knew what His Lordship would say, so I did not tell him," Mr. Bennett explained. "There was a cottage empty at the end of the village, and Nanny moved into it."

"And you did not tell Simon about it?" Kasia asked.

Mr. Bennett looked uncomfortable.

"I was hoping he would settle down with his Tutor. I was afraid that Nanny might somehow interfere in his lessons."

Kasia did not say anything.

Mr. Bennett had been, she thought, as stupid with Simon as everyone else.

What he needed was affection and love.

It was something that had been missing in his life ever since his Mother had died.

Then, when he most needed her, his Nanny had been taken from him.

They drove towards the cottage which Kasia was told was at the end of the village.

She thought Simon was trying hard to contain his excitement at the thought of seeing his Nanny again.

But he was unpredictable.

She could not help praying that she had not made a mistake.

"Rose Cottage", as it was called, was thatched and pretty.

At the same time, like a great many other cottages in the village, it needed paint.

There were also cracks in several of the window-panes.

As Kasia drew up the pony-cart Simon jumped out.

"Shall I knock and see if Nanny is inside?" he asked.

"Yes, of course," Kasia said. "I will see if I can find somebody to hold the pony."

It was old, and not likely to wander off.

At the same time she thought it would be wise to have somebody to look after it.

There was a boy playing in a garden on the other side of the road and she called to him:

"I will give you three pence if you will look after this pony while I am inside the cottage."

"Oi'll see 'e don' go 'way," the boy said eagerly.

By the time she had walked up the path the front door was open and Simon had gone inside.

Kasia could see an elderly woman with white hair had her arms around him.

Then he was talking nineteen to the dozen after she had sat down in a chair to listen to him.

"They were horrid, nasty people, Nanny," Simon was saying. "They would not let me do anything I wanted to do, and when I ran away to try to find you they said they would beat me if I did it again!"

"That was very wrong of them," Nanny said. "I was afraid you would miss me."

"I cried and cried," Simon said, "but they would not let you come back."

"I think you can come back now, Nanny," Kasia said from the door.

Nanny looked up in surprise and Simon said:

"This is my new Governess, Nanny. She is very nice, and tells me stories like you used to do."

Kasia walked into the cottage.

"Do not get up, Nanny," she said quickly as the old woman tried to rise from her chair. "I have only just discovered how much Simon needs you, and if you will allow me to do so, I will ask the Duke if you may come and live at the Castle."

"They said as how Simon was too old to have a Nanny," the elderly woman answered.

"He is too young to be without a Mother," Kasia said simply, and Nanny understood.

When they went down to luncheon she let Simon tell the Duke how he had tried to search for Nanny after they sent her away and how he had found her again.

The Duke listened. Then he said to Kasia:

"I suppose this is your doing."

"Nanny is prepared to come and live at the Castle, if you will permit it," Kasia said simply.

The Duke's lips twisted for a moment.

"I can hardly say no!"

"Why should you want to say no?" Kasia asked. "I believe she is very important to Simon."

"I want Nanny, I want her very much," Simon said, "and I also want Miss Watson to stay with me."

"Which, of course, I am going to do," Kasia said.

"Very well," the Duke agreed, "I will send a carriage for Nanny this afternoon."

Kasia smiled at him.

"I hoped that was what you would do."

"I have a feeling I have little choice," the Duke replied.

Because Simon was so delighted at having his Nanny back he had plenty to say at luncheon.

Kasia thought afterwards that he and she had managed to keep the Duke laughing.

"He must really be bored," she told herself, "and longing to be in London with all the beautiful women, like Lady Julie."

However he showed no sign of being bored.

Once again he said he would like them to have tea with him, although it might be rather later than it had been yesterday.

"I am going to the farms," he explained. "I did two this morning and there are two more waiting for me this afternoon."

"I would like to see the little lambs," Simon said unexpectedly.

"Very well," the Duke replied, "you and Miss Watson shall accompany me. You can look at the lambs, the chickens and the calves while I talk to the farmers."

"That is something new to do," Simon said.

"I only hope," the Duke replied, "that I am not interfering with your lessons."

Kasia knew he was teasing her, and she replied:

"Not at all, Your Grace. Simon must learn about

country matters, which are all round him, as well as those subjects which are only to be found in books."

"I found the picture of King William all by myself today," Simon said proudly, "and Miss Watson gave me a prize of a four-penny piece."

"Which of course is bribery and corruption," the Duke said in an aside to Kasia.

"On the contrary, it was as important as the laurel wreath at the Olympic Games!" Kasia retorted.

The Duke laughed.

. . . .

They drove off in a Phaeton with Simon sitting between the two grown-ups.

The Duke pointed out to them various landmarks that were familiar to him from the time when he had been at the Castle as a boy.

There was a Mill which was not working at the moment, but he said he was determined to get it into operation as soon as possible.

There was what had once been a race-course, but had fallen into disrepair during the war. He was arranging to put it into order again.

Then they saw in the distance a tall tower which he told Simon had once been a Watch-Tower for the Earls who had then lived in the Castle.

That was also in need of attention.

"You are not to go near it," the Duke said, "until I have had time to restore it."

"Were there soldiers in the Watch-Tower?" Simon asked.

"I suspect they were Archers," the Duke said,

"and they would have shot down any enemy who came near them."

"With bows and arrows," Kasia said in case Simon did not understand.

"That reminds me," the Duke said. "When I was a boy Archery contests took place here and it is something I would like to revive."

"My Father taught me how to use a bow and arrow," Kasia said, "and I think if you bought a small one for Simon, it is something he would enjoy."

"Who shall I shoot?" Simon asked.

"A target!" the Duke said firmly, "and nothing else! Then if you hit the bulls-eye you will receive a prize."

"Oh, please let me have a bow and arrow," Simon pleaded. "I want to win lots more prizes, then I can go shopping."

"You have had your pocket-money," Kasia said.

"Oh, yes, of course!" Simon said as if he had forgotten.

"It is something I should have remembered," the Duke said, "and of course, Miss Watson, I am very contrite."

Kasia smiled.

"You must not blame yourself," she said. "After all, you have no children of your own. However, I think your relatives have been somewhat mean."

"That is the right way to describe them," the Duke said. "I am determined that is something I will never be."

He spoke so fervently that Kasia guessed he

too had suffered from their meanness in the past.

She remembered someone telling her that he had been quite poor before he became the Duke.

Talking of money made her think of her own and that reminded her of Lord Stefelton.

She gave a little shiver and the Duke asked:

"What is upsetting you?"

She was so surprised that he should be aware of what she was feeling that she looked at him, and he said:

"I feel I can read your thoughts, Miss Watson, and your eyes are very expressive."

"Whatever it is, I hope you will not know what I am thinking," Kasia replied, "because that would be very upsetting."

"Why?" the Duke asked.

There was no answer to this, and she remained silent.

Only when they returned home after an extremely interesting afternoon with the farmers did the Duke say:

"I would like to talk to you after dinner, Miss Watson. I have given orders that Simon is to dine with you, although I think it would be better if we all dined together."

As if he had suddenly thought of it, he exclaimed:

"Yes – that is a much better idea! Then I can be certain that the boy is being fed as he should be at his age."

"But I am sure Your Grace has no wish to dine so early," Kasia said.

"We will make it seven o'clock," the Duke said,

"which after all, is the right time to dine in the country. Then Simon can be in bed by seven-thirty."

"I would like that," Simon smiled, "because you have such scrumptious things to eat! I hate bread and milk, and Miss Watson said I was far too old for that sort of baby food."

"Miss Watson is right," the Duke agreed. "So tonight you can enjoy yourself as I expect there will be the usual four or more courses for dinner. You will soon get as fat as a small pig!"

Simon laughed.

"If I ride *Princess* very fast, Uncle Darcy, I shall get as thin as you."

"That is extremely good thinking," the Duke said, "and I agree with you."

Then as he looked at Kasia she knew quite well he had deliberately made it possible to dine with her, and not be alone.

'I must not flatter myself that it is because he wants to talk to me,' she thought. 'It is more a case of "any port in a storm", and he does not like being alone.'

At the same time, she felt a strange excitement rising within her.

She knew she wanted to dine with the Duke, and she wanted to talk to him.

'When Simon has gone to bed,' she thought, 'we can talk and talk, as we did last night.'

As if the Duke knew what she was thinking, he met her eyes.

Then it was almost impossible for either of them to look away.

CHAPTER SIX

Simon pushed back his plate and got up from the breakfast-table.

"I am going to help Mr. Bennett with the wages," he said.

"That is very kind of you," Kasia smiled. "He said you were a great help yesterday."

"I will not be very long," Simon said. "Where will you be?"

"In the Music-Room," Kasia replied.

"Oh, that is good!" he said.

He bent forward, kissed her on the cheek, then walked towards the door.

As it shut behind him, the Duke asked:

"What is all this?"

Kasia smiled.

"I thought you would be surprised," she said, "but as Simon is so keen on money, I suggested he helped Mr. Bennett count out the wages. It is quite a long job at the moment with so many workmen here."

The Duke was staring as if he did not understand, and she went on:

"You know that Mr. Bennett counts out each man's money in silver and it means a lot of work. He said that Simon was good at it, and he could hardly believe he could have mastered the different coins so quickly."

"So that is Arithmetic!" the Duke said.

"Of course," Kasia smiled, "and I will tell you something which is even more exciting."

"What is that?" he asked.

"I remembered reading that Musicians are often innately good Mathematicians . ."

The Duke was listening, and she went on:

". . . Yesterday I played Simon some tunes on the piano and he managed to pick them out almost immediately with one finger."

"You never cease to amaze me, Miss Watson!" the Duke declared. "As, indeed you have done ever since you came here."

"Has it really been a week?" Kasia asked. "So much has happened that I can hardly believe it!"

"Neither can I," the Duke agreed, "and that is why I want to talk to you."

There was a deep note in his voice which made her look up at him.

They both appeared to be speaking without words.

Then the door opened and the Butler came in.

"The Foreman of the Builders wants to speak to Your Grace," he said to the Duke.

"That is the man I sent for," the Duke said. "Have you put him in the Study?"

"Yes, Your Grace."

"Tell him I will come at once," the Duke added.

114

The Butler walked towards the door.

The Duke finished his coffee and got up.

"I am afraid I shall not be in for luncheon today," he said to Kasia, "since I have to go with this man to see one of the outlying farms. The house is in such a terrible state of disrepair that it might be best to pull it down and start again."

"Simon and I will miss you," Kasia said, "but I hope you will be back in time for tea."

"You can be sure of it!" the Duke said. "Take care of yourselves."

"We are riding after luncheon," Kasia said, "and Simon is thrilled that you are allowing him to ride *Dragonfly*."

The Duke smiled.

"*Dragonfly* is faster than *Princess* but equally well-trained and perfectly safe unless anything out of the ordinary occurs."

"I will try to make sure that does not happen," Kasia replied.

The Duke looked at her again and seemed about to say something.

Then he changed his mind.

He went from the Breakfast-Room and Kasia knew she would miss him.

It had been such fun these past few days, having both luncheon and dinner with him.

Although she had always been afraid he might find Simon and her boring, he had shown no sign of it.

In fact, every meal seemed to be one of interest, and also unending laughter.

"It has also been very exciting!" she added to herself.

When luncheon came, she missed the Duke.

Simon chatted away about the money with which he had helped Mr. Bennett, and also the music which had followed.

"I want to play with two hands, like you," he said.

"You will do that very soon," Kasia promised. "Then we will arrange a musical evening and you shall play for your Uncle."

"He will be surprised if I can play like you!" Simon said.

"He will also be delighted, and very impressed to see how clever you have become."

"Clever enough to ride on a fast horse!" Simon said triumphantly.

Dragonfly was a very good-looking horse.

When Simon was mounted on him Kasia thought it was a pity that the Duke was not there to see how attractive he looked.

They set off in their usual way, first into the paddocks, then riding over the flat ground beyond them.

"I am going faster and faster!" Simon shouted.

Kasia had to admit he was riding very well and her own horse had to exert itself to keep up with him.

They rode until they came to a small clump of trees.

Then they had to pull in their horses so as to go through it in single file.

There was some ground on the other side on which they had ridden before.

They were quite a long way from the Castle by now, but Kasia thought there was no point in returning too early and having to wait for the Duke.

Then, as Simon went ahead of her through a copse, suddenly from behind the trees two men appeared.

Almost before Kasia could realise what was happening, they seized *Dragonfly*'s bridle.

As they did so two other men were standing beside her horse with their hands on the bridle.

"Who are you? What do you want?" Kasia asked.

"Ye'll larn soon 'nough!" one of the men answered in a rough voice.

To Kasia's horror she was pulled out of the saddle onto the ground.

As she landed she heard Simon give a cry and saw that he too was being dragged off his horse.

"What are you doing?" she tried to ask.

A gag was tied over her mouth, and at the same time a rope was wound round her.

It pinioned her arms to her sides.

She tried to struggle, but it was hopeless.

A minute later a cloth was thrown over her head so that she could not see.

She found herself being picked up and carried for what seemed some distance.

She thought they must now be out of the wood.

She was sure this was so when she was put down rather roughly in what she guessed was a cart.

She was then aware that Simon was being placed beside her, and the cart started off.

As it was impossible either to see or to speak, she could only listen.

She thought the cart must be a wagon like those the farmers used, and was drawn by one horse.

'Who are they? What are they doing? Why were they waiting for us?' she wondered desperately.

Then she felt sure that, whoever they were, they had taken Simon prisoner in order to demand a ransom from the Duke.

It was something her Father had always been afraid might happen to her.

However nothing of the kind had in fact ever happened.

Nevertheless he had always insisted that the Night-Watchman in whichever house they were, should be armed.

When they travelled she knew although her Father did not tell her so, that there was always a loaded revolver beside his bed.

Since the war, men were returning from the Forces without a pension and without work.

This had given rise to much more crime on the roads and in the Cities.

In Highwayman fashion, robbers, rogues and men who were simply hungry, extorted money from anyone they thought was rich.

She wondered what the Duke would do.

If they asked for ransom money for Simon, would he try to rescue them?

Then she remembered despairingly how large the Estate was, and how wild and sparsely inhabited the country-side.

118

If their Kidnappers hid them cleverly, it would be impossible for the Duke to have any idea where they were.

On and on the wagon in which she and Simon were travelling bumped over the rough, uneven ground.

It made Kasia sure they were being taken to some isolated spot where they would never be found.

She felt herself tremble with fear of what lay ahead.

It must have been half-an-hour or perhaps longer when the wagon came to a standstill.

She was pulled roughly from the back of the cart and lifted up in a man's arms.

She was sure from the movements beside her that another man was moving Simon.

The man carrying her walked a little way in silence until he said:

"Ye'll 'ave ter gimme a 'and wi' 'er up t'steps."

" 'Er looks light enough t'me," another voice answered.

"Gimme a 'and!" the first one said furiously.

With one man holding her shoulders and the other her ankles, Kasia was carried up some steep steps.

She assumed at first they were outside.

Then as they climbed higher and higher she knew she was inside a building.

Up and up they went, and she understood why the man who had been carrying her first, did not want to continue alone.

When the steps came to an end the two men

walked across what sounded like a wooden floor before they put her down.

It was then to her relief that the cloth was pulled from her head.

For a moment after the darkness, and also because it had been difficult to breathe, Kasia could only blink.

Then she realised she was sitting on the floor in what seemed like a small room.

Standing looking at her were two coarse-looking men.

She was sure from their appearance and the way they had spoken that they were from some Town or City.

She did not know why she felt this, but they did not appear to her like countrymen.

She looked hastily around to see if Simon was with her.

To her relief he had just been brought into the room.

The man who was carrying him had him over his shoulder as a Fireman might have done.

He put Simon down next to Kasia and one of the other men said:

"Ye be careful wiv 'im! 'E's worf good money!"

The man who had carried Simon in laughed.

"Tha's wot we 'opes, and Oi'd rather 'ave 'im in me pocket, than me back!"

The cover was lifted from Simon's head.

"Do us turn 'em loose?" the man asked who had carried him, "or leave 'em be?"

"Let 'em be loose," another man answered. " 'Sides, 'er's gotta write th' letter fer us."

He pointed at Kasia as he spoke and the other man nodded his head.

"Oi left th' paper an' ink downstairs," he said.

He walked across the room, and Kasia could hear his footsteps going down the long flight of stairs up which they had come.

The two men who were there took the gags from her mouth and Simon's.

They then pulled off the ropes with which they had tied down their arms.

"Why are you doing this?" Simon asked when he could speak, "and who are you?"

"That be a good question, Sonny!" one of the men answered, "an' if ye be'ave yerself we're yer friends, but if ye don't, we're yer enemies."

"Why have you brought me here?" Simon asked.

The man put his finger to his nose in an age-old gesture.

"Nah that's askin', but ye'll soon find aht, when Bill comes back."

"I am sure you have no right to bring us here!" Simon said. "My Uncle will be very angry."

"We 'opes as 'e'll be very worried," one of the men answered, "in fac', we're bettin' 'e will be."

"I think, if I am not mistaken," Kasia said in what she hoped was a well controlled voice, "you have brought us here to ask for money."

"Now ain't that clever of ye!" one of the men said in a mocking tone. "Oo'd 'ave believed, lookin' so pretty, ye'd 'it th' bull's-eye first time?"

As he spoke there was the sound of Bill who had gone down the stairs coming back.

The men turned their heads to watch for his appearance.

He was puffing as he came into the room.

"Them stairs'll gimme an 'eart-attack!" he complained. "Now, let's get on wiv it. Th' sooner we 'as th' money an' gets orf 'ome, th' better!"

"Oi agrees wi' ye," one of the other men replied.

Carrying the paper and the ink-pot Bill squatted down beside Kasia.

There was also, she saw, a rather dirty quill pen.

"Now, write a note to 'Is Nibs," he said, "an' tell 'im if 'e wants t'see th' boy again, 'e's gotta cough up two thousand quid, an' we wants it in cash!"

"Where will you wait for him to give it to you?" Kasia asked.

Bill laughed and it was an unpleasant sound.

"Oi ain't so nit-witted as that! Ye can tell 'im ter leave it inside th' broken door of th' old Mill."

Kasia remembered the Duke pointing out the Mill when they were driving and she nodded.

"An' tell 'im when th' money's there an' no one waitin' to catch us, to put a white flag up on th' top o' th' Castle."

"That's right," one of the other men said. "When us sees that we'll go t'th' Mill."

"Jus' one o' us!" another man said, pointing with his finger at Kasia. "An' if 'Is Nibs don't put it up, or ther's any 'hanky-panky', ye'll both die! Make that clear!"

"I will write what you tell me," Kasia said, "but I think you are all behaving very badly."

Bill laughed scornfully.

"Badly! Wot's bad be th' Dook's got money – bags o' it – an' us got nothin'! That's wot's bad!"

"Ow, come on, let 'er get on wiv' it," one of the other men said, "Luke'll be 'ere in a minute an' 'e can take t'letter t'th' old Mill."

" 'E'll walk quick enough," Bill replied. " 'E'll 'ave t'take th' wagon back ter where us took it from."

He spoke impatiently as he put down the paper and pen beside Kasia.

She was sitting up with her back against the wall as she said:

"It is going to be difficult to write like this. Have you a box or something I can rest the paper on?"

"Ow dear – Oi jes' remembered! We ain't smartened it up fer Yer Ladyship!" the man said mockingly.

But Bill said:

"Let 'er do it right. Oi'll find somethin' downstairs."

He started to go down the steps again.

Kasia looked towards Simon.

To her relief, he was not looking very frightened, just staring from one man to another as if he could hardly believe what was happening.

She put out a hand towards him and he said:

"This is like a story, Miss Watson, isn't it?"

Kasia smiled at him.

"Exactly! And of course we have to do what these men tell us to do."

"That's right," one of the men said. "Yer've got the right idea, an' if yer a Governess, which is wot us were told, yer gets full marks!"

"Who told you I was a Governess?" Kasia enquired.

"Oi ain't givin' away no names," the man answered. "That could get us inter trouble!"

There was the sound of Bill who had gone downstairs coming back.

A few seconds later he came in through the door carrying a wooden box, and said:

"There y'are, a table straight from Buckingham Palace! 'Oo could ask fer more?"

Kasia put the paper down on it, and one of the men added the ink-pot.

As she picked up the pen Bill said:

"Nah, ye be careful wot ye says. No 'ints as t'where we be, or Oi'll knock yer 'ead orf! An' that goes fer th' boy too!"

There was a ferociousness in the way he spoke that was frightening and Kasia said quietly:

"You can dictate it, word for word, if you like."

"Ow, get on wiv it!" Bill said. "Yer tell th' Dook wot 'e's got to 'ear, an' pay up quick – that's wot matters."

"Aye, yer right," another man agreed. "That's all us wants."

"Very well," Kasia said.

She started the letter, which was far easier now that she had a box on which to write.

124

She was wondering how she could give the Duke a hint as to where they were hidden, seeing that she did not know herself.

Then as if he had been wondering the same thing, Simon said:

"I know where we are! We are in the Watch-Tower and it is dangerous – very dangerous!"

The men looked at each other as if they were surprised by what he had said.

Then one of them answered:

"Yer right, an' we shouldn't be 'ere, an' th' sooner us can leave 'ere, th' better!"

"An' if us 'as ter wait fer our money, it might collapse round yer, an' ye'll be buried in it."

Simon turned towards Kasia.

"Uncle Darcy said it was very dangerous, and that I must never come here."

"I know," Kasia replied, "and I am sure he will be very angry that we have been brought here."

"Never mind 'bout that!" Bill interrupted.

"Jus' ye get on wiv yer writin'. Th' sooner 'e coughs up the money, the sooner ye can go 'ome. If 'e don't – we'll lock yer in an' no one'll find yer."

He took a pistol from his pocket as he spoke.

"Them as be dead don't talk!" he said. "An' talks wot Oi don't want to 'ear."

Kasia thought Bill was obviously the ring-leader of the men.

She was sure of this when a few minutes later the man called Luke, who had been putting back the horse and wagon, joined them.

"That's good!" Bill answered. "Now we've got

'nother errand fer yer t'do, as ye be th' one as runs fastest."

"Oi mighta known Oi'd be a-doin' all th' dirty work!" Luke moaned.

"It won't seem so dirty when 'ems coins be jinglin' in yer pocket!" Bill replied.

Kasia was writing quickly.

At the same time she was wondering frantically how she could tell the Duke where they were without the men being aware of what she had done.

She was quite certain that if she put in anything like "We are *Watch*ing for your reply", they would be smart enough to know what she was trying to do.

She sent up a prayer, feeling that only her Guardian Angel could help them in the situation in which she and Simon found themselves.

"Help me . . help me to show him . . where . . we are," she begged.

Almost as if she had a direct answer, she had an idea.

She went over carefully what she had written, finished the letter and signed her name.

Then she handed it to Bill who was standing watching her.

"Is that what you wanted me to write?" she asked.

He took it from her and read aloud what she had written.

He mispronounced some of the words, but she realised that he could read.

She felt the other men would not find it easy.

Bill paused once or twice when he found something difficult.

She knew it was due more to the thickness of the pen and the cheapness of the paper than to her hand-writing.

Finally he said:

"That's orl right. 'Er's signed 'er name, but it be one Oi ain't never 'eard of afore."

It was then that Kasia gave a little gasp.

She realised that because she had been so intent on surreptitiously giving the Duke a hint of where they were, she had signed 'Kasia' Watson, instead of 'Kate'.

It was stupid of her, but she thought it was of no particular importance.

It would certainly be a mistake for the men to know she was disguising herself in any way.

"Is the letter all right?" she asked.

"Ye've made clear wot we wants," Bill replied, "an' Oi 'opes fer yer sake as 'e'll put th' money where ye've told 'im to."

"I have written what you told me to say," Kasia replied.

"Now it's up ter 'im," Luke said, "an' Oi likes th' idea of th' white flag on top o' th' Castle."

"It means 'e's surrenderin', don't it!" Bill said with a gruff laugh.

"That is something Uncle Darcy never did in the war," Simon said unexpectedly, "so he may want to fight you."

"If 'e wants ter do that, us'll be ready fer 'im, eh, boys?" Bill retorted.

He patted the pocket into which he had put the pistol as he spoke.

As the other men did the same, Kasia thought with her heart sinking that they were all armed.

She only hoped the Duke would not approach them unarmed.

Then she told herself that anyway it was unlikely he would understand what she had tried to convey to him.

She was beginning to wish she had not done so, but had just written what they wanted her to write.

After all, it was not a tremendous amount of money they were demanding.

There would certainly be that amount of cash in the Office.

Apart from the wages to be paid on Friday, to so many men, she was certain that the Duke would have extra funds to pay for the necessary materials.

Also for the animals and machinery for which the Farmers were asking.

Bill took one last look at the letter.

He then folded the paper and handing it back to Kasia ordered:

"Put 'is name on th' outside!"

"Yes, of course," Kasia said.

She wrote in capital letters:

"TO HIS GRACE THE DUKE OF DREGHORNE."

She handed back the letter to Bill.

"Right, Luke," he said, "orf ye goes, an' be careful no one sees ye shove it frough th' door of th' old Mill, or push it through th' winder."

Kasia gave a little cry.

"Supposing nobody happens to find it? It might be months before the Duke has any idea of what has happened to us and what you want."

" 'Er's got a point there, Bill," one of the men said.

"Oi ain't goin' up t'th' Castle t' get meself caught!" Luke said.

"I do not see why there should be any trouble," Kasia replied before Bill could speak. "You could just be handing in a note at the door. The footman will take it and no one will know what is written in it, until the Duke opens it and reads it."

The men were silent and she said:

"He can tie a scarf round his neck so that it does not reveal all his face, and give him a hat to pull over his forehead."

She paused a moment and then went on:

"The letter will take some time to reach His Grace and by then Luke will be half-way back here."

"That be sense, sheer commonsense!" Bill said. "An' as soon as us gets th' money us can be back where we comes from, an' that's all that matters."

"Oi don't like it!" Luke said. "Oi'm afraid o' goin' up t'th' front door an' 'avin' them servants starin' at Oi."

"There are so many workmen going in and out of the doors at the moment," Kasia said, "that I am sure no one will take any particular notice of you."

She looked at them to make sure they were listening to her and then continued:

"But if it will make you any happier, go to the Service Entrance. They will certainly think there that you are one of the workmen. Tell them that the letter for His Grace has to go to him at once."

"That's more like it!" Bill said. "Ye go to th' Service Entrance, Luke, an' that be th' right place fer ye."

Luke, who was a crafty-looking little man, said:

"Orl right, Oi'll do as ye say, Bill, but Oi on'y 'opes as Oi'm not runnin' into a trap!"

"If it is, this clever young lady knows what's comin' to 'er!" Bill said.

He gave Kasia as he spoke an unpleasant look that made her shiver.

Then Simon said:

"Uncle Darcy said he would be home for tea. He will be wondering where we are."

"That's jes' wot us be goin' t'tell 'im," Bill said, "an' I s'pose, young jackanapes, ye was 'spectin' t'ave a cup o' tea. Well, that's somethin' ye ain't 'avin', as we ain't got none."

He laughed, as if at his own joke.

"If yer 'ungry," he finished, "it'll make ye all th' keener to 'urry orf 'ome when yer Uncle pays up."

He turned to Kasia to say nastily:

"Pity ye didn't put that in! If 'e takes too long, th' 'ungrier ye'll both get!"

He laughed again.

Then crossing the room, he started to go down the stairs.

The two other men followed him, looking back

as they did so at Simon with what she thought was an unpleasant expression in their eyes.

The last man to leave shut the wooden door behind him.

She wondered if he would lock it.

As there was no sound of a key being turned in the lock, she supposed there was no key there.

As soon as they had gone Simon jumped up.

"They are bad and wicked!" he said. "They have made us prisoners, just like two people in a story."

He did not sound frightened, but rather excited by it, and Kasia said:

"Come close to me and I will tell you a secret."

Simon moved quickly to her side.

"What is it?" he asked.

In a whisper, although Kasia was quite certain that by now the men were out of ear-shot, she said:

"I have made a secret sign in the letter which I hope will tell your Uncle where we are. Now we have to pray, and pray very hard, that he will understand."

CHAPTER SEVEN

The Duke arrived back at the Castle just after five o'clock and walked quickly into the Drawing-Room.

The words "I am sorry to be late" were on his lips as he opened the door.

To his surprise there was no one there.

He thought they must have finished tea and left, but when he looked at the table he saw that the food was untouched.

He rang the bell and the Butler came hurrying to his side.

"Where are Master Simon and Miss Watson?"

"They've not yet returned, Your Grace."

"Not returned?" the Duke said looking at the clock. "Surely they are very late?"

"I were wondering what had happened, Your Grace."

"Well find out if they are in the stables," the Duke ordered.

The Butler went away to obey his instructions, and he walked across the room to the window.

He was thinking of Kasia as he had been thinking

of her nearly all the afternoon.

He had admitted to himself a day or so ago that he was in love; more in love than he had ever been in his life.

But he was not certain what to do about it.

He knew that in his new position as the Duke the family would be expecting him to marry someone whose blood equalled his own and who was of Social importance.

That he should stoop to marry one of his employees was quite unthinkable.

He could imagine only too well the horror amongst his relatives.

Moreover, apart from anything else, they could make Kasia's life unbearable.

At the same time, he had not been with her for a week without realising how innocent and unspoiled she was.

He was quite sure she had no idea how the Beauties of the *Beau Monde* like Lady Julie, behaved.

Or the depths of depravity to which they were prepared to sink when they desired a man.

"What am I to do?" he asked himself. "What the devil can I do?"

It was a question that seemed to have been ringing in his ears now for a very long time.

He had realised he was falling in love almost as soon as he had set eyes on that fascinating, heart-shaped little face, with its two large eyes.

Eyes which told him she had the innocence of a child, as well as a star-like glitter which he found irresistible.

He knew too that he had never before met a woman he found so interesting.

She was intelligent and, what was extraordinary, so well read and well educated.

Only someone who was exceptionally clever, he thought, could have understood the problem of Simon and settled it in her own way.

The change in the boy was astounding.

He knew that his relatives, when they saw him again, would find it incredible.

How could he be the same child they had sent away, one after another, because he was so unruly that they could not control him.

The Duke had to admit that it was not he who had performed this miracle, but Simon's Governess.

"Governess! Governess!"

The word seemed to repeat itself over and over again in his brain.

She was someone he had hired; someone he was paying for her service.

How could he marry her?

Yet he knew he could not offer to pay her for something very different.

If he suggested it, he knew she would be shocked and frightened.

How could he do that to someone he loved?

Someone who had begun to haunt him so that he could not sleep at night, but lay awake wanting her.

"I love her!" he admitted again. "God, what am I to do about it?"

He heard someone coming into the Drawing-Room and turned round eagerly.

But it was only Dawson the Butler coming back.

"I'm afraid, Your Grace, it's bad news!" he said.

"Bad news?" the Duke repeated.

"The horse Miss Watson was riding has come back to th' stables without its rider, and there's no sign of *Dragonfly*!"

"There must have been an accident!" the Duke exclaimed. "Has anyone any idea of where they went?"

Dawson shook his head.

"No, Your Grace. They just set off in th' usual way after luncheon, riding through th' paddocks."

"I will go in search of them," the Duke said.

It seemed strange that Miss Watson, when she rode so well, should have been thrown.

But that is what he thought must have happened because the horse had returned alone, and Simon must have stayed with her.

Perhaps she had broken a leg or something worse.

The Duke felt as if a knife was turning in his heart.

He walked towards the door intending to go to the stables, but Dawson stopped him.

"There's a letter just arrived for Your Grace," he said. "The man who handed it in at th' Service Entrance said 'twas very urgent."

The Duke was about to say that he would see to it when he returned.

Then it struck him that perhaps, if it was very urgent, it concerned Miss Watson and Simon.

Without speaking he put out his hand and Dawson placed the letter in it.

The Duke opened it, then stiffened into immobility.

Then he read:

"Your Grace,

Simon and I have been taken prisoner by some men who demand a ransom of £2,000 in cash.

They want you To put the money in The broken door of The Old Mill. Then fly a white flag from The mast at The Top of The Castle to show it is There.

If The money is not forthcoming, they have Threatened That you will see neither of us again.

They told me to ask you to PAY UP at once.

Yours regretfully,
Kasia Watson."

The Duke read through twice what Kasia had written.

Then he went into action.

It gradually grew darker in the room at the top of the Watch-Tower.

Simon moved so that he was sitting close to Kasia, and rested his head against her shoulder.

"I am hungry," he said.

"I know you must be," Kasia replied, "and I can only hope that your Uncle will not be too long about paying these horrible men, or saving us."

"Do you think he will understand what you have tried to tell him?" Simon asked.

"I had to do it very, very carefully," Kasia explained, "but I thought if he read it he would think it strange that I had crossed the small 't's at the top in the way you would cross a capital 'T'."

Simon did not say anything and she went on:

"Then when I wrote that the men had said he must pay up, I wrote those two words very large, and underlined them."

"Then do you think he will understand that we are up in the Watch-Tower?" Simon asked as if he was working it out for himself.

"I am praying he will," Kasia said, "and that is what you must do too."

"He will not hear us praying," Simon argued.

"In India," Kasia said, "the Indians believe in the Power of Thought."

She smiled at him and then went on:

"I have read in books that a man will know that his Father has died three-hundred miles away from where he is without there having been any communication, except that he *knows* in his mind it is true."

"Then we must send a message to Uncle Darcy's mind," Simon said.

"That is what I am trying to do," Kasia answered, "and you must help me."

"How?" Simon asked.

"Think of your Uncle, try to see him standing in the Drawing-Room or in his Study, and keep saying 'Watch-Tower, Watch-Tower' in your heart."

"I will try," Simon said. "I will try very, very hard. I do not like being here."

"Neither do I," Kasia answered, and she pulled Simon a little closer to her.

Later, when she realised he had fallen asleep, she took off her riding-jacket and made him a pillow for his head.

As she moved him down onto it he did not open his eyes, but murmured sleepily:

"Watch . . Tower . . Watch . . Tower . . ."

It was what she kept saying herself.

The Tower had become hot and stuffy and she walked across to the window and opened it as wide as it would go.

The stars were coming out overhead.

The moon which had been behind the clouds was now creeping up the sky.

It was casting a silvery light all over the land.

The shadows were long and dark, and Kasia thought how uninhabited and barren it looked.

It was a clever place to hide because there was no reason for anyone to come past the Watch-Tower.

The fields all around it had not been ploughed or seeded.

She had a terrifying feeling that the Duke would not understand what she had written.

Also, in the interests of other people, he would not give in to kidnappers.

If they succeeded in obtaining money from him, as soon as it was spent, they would kidnap another child.

She felt herself trembling at the thought that if she and Simon were not rescued, they would be left to starve.

Or perhaps those evil men downstairs would kill them before they went in search of other prey.

"Oh . . God . . please . . God . . let him . . understand!"

Because she could not bear to go on looking at the empty fields, she went back to sit down beside Simon.

He had been very brave, she thought, where most children might have screamed and cried, or clung to her.

"He will be very brave when he grows up," she told herself, "just like his Uncle."

Even to think of the Duke was to conjure up a picture of him riding on his black stallion.

Sitting at the top of the dining-table.

Standing in front of the fireplace as he laughed at something that had been said.

"He is so handsome and so clever," she told herself, and her heart turned a somersault.

She felt as if she reached out to him with both her hands.

She remembered how their eyes had met this morning when he told her there was something he wanted to talk to her about.

She wondered what he wanted to tell her.

She was half afraid he was going to say that he had to return to London, and she must cope with Simon alone.

She added something else to her prayer.

"Let him stay . . please, God . . let him . . stay and help him to . . find us . . soon."

She prayed with such fervency that she put her

fingers up to her eyes as if it helped her to concentrate.

Then she was aware of a sound.

It was as if something was scratching and she thought with a sudden terror that it was rats.

She had always been frightened of rats.

She realised they would doubtless infest the empty Tower which no one ever visited.

The sound grew louder, and she thought there must be a large number of them.

Stories she had heard of them biting babies in their cots and attacking grown-ups flashed through her mind.

She thought wildly that if she screamed the men downstairs would come and save her and Simon.

She took her fingers from her eyes and was about to get to her feet.

Then she was aware that the moonlight which was pouring through the window was suddenly obscured.

For a moment she could not think what was happening.

There was a movement and a leg came through the open window which she sensed, rather than saw.

It was followed by a man's body and it was then she sprang to her feet.

It was the Duke.

She knew instinctively that it was the Duke without seeing his face.

She flung herself against him as his feet touched the floor.

As she did so his arms went round her.

She was about to speak and cry out for joy.

Then his lips found hers.

He was holding her against him and it was impossible to breathe.

She only knew a rapture that shot through her like lightning with sensations she had never experienced before.

The Duke kissed her fiercely, demandingly, then raised his head and whispered:

"Do not make a sound! How many men are there?"

"F.four," Kasia murmured, "and they are . . armed."

"They have not hurt you?"

"No, no, we are all right, and Simon is asleep."

The Duke moved a little further into the room, still without taking his arms from Kasia.

In the moonlight coming through the window he could see Simon lying on the floor.

It was then, when Kasia would have spoken again that the Duke whispered:

"Wake Simon, and get behind the door."

She wanted to ask him questions, but he had turned away from her.

Drawing a pistol from his pocket, he fired it out of the window.

The noise of the explosion woke Simon and as Kasia pulled him to his feet, he exclaimed:

"Uncle Darcy! I knew you would come!"

The Duke did not reply and Kasia, knowing she must obey him, pulled Simon towards the door.

"Open it," the Duke said quietly.

She did so and pulled it back so that she and Simon were out of sight behind it.

It was then they heard shots coming from below.

Kasia knew that the Duke's men, who had come with him, were firing at Bill and his accomplices.

Now someone was coming up the stairs, the boards creaking beneath his feet.

It was, as Kasia soon saw, Bill who burst into the room, holding a pistol in his hand.

It was pointing at the spot where Kasia and Simon had been sitting before the Duke told them to move.

As he took a step forward the Duke fired, the bullet hitting him in the right arm.

The pistol fell on the floor with a clatter.

"Ye've killed me! Ye've killed me!" Bill screamed.

"You are alive, unfortunately," the Duke answered. "Go downstairs and join your villainous gang."

Bill, clutching his injured arm, turned round.

He knew it was no use arguing against the voice of authority.

The Duke picked up the pistol the man had dropped.

The shooting below had stopped and he said to Kasia:

"Stay here until I call you, but I think now we will all be able to go home."

"That was a good shot, Uncle Darcy!" Simon said admiringly. "Can I have the pistol?"

The Duke looked to see if there were any more bullets, removed those that remained, and handed it to Simon.

"Guard Kasia," he said.

Then he was following Bill down the stairs.

Kasia feeling as if her legs would no longer carry her sat down on the floor.

The Duke saved them!

She might have known he would.

At the same time, the relief was so intense as to be almost overwhelming.

Her prayers had reached him and he had understood.

He had come, as she had hoped and trusted he would.

"I love . . him! I . . love him!" she told herself.

She felt as if the sun was lighting their prison in a blaze of glory.

It must only have been a few minutes before they heard the Duke call out:

"Come down! It is all over."

The sound of his voice was like a clarion call.

Kasia got to her feet and picking up her jacket put it on.

She saw as she did so that Simon was already running down the stairs, even though it was difficult to see his way in the darkness.

She wanted to warn him to be cautious.

But the only thing that mattered was that the Duke was waiting for them at the bottom.

Simon was already beside the Duke, holding his pistol.

As Kasia reached the last steps, the Duke put out his hand to help her down them.

At the touch of his fingers she felt herself quiver.

As she looked up at him she thought in the moonlight no man could look more handsome.

He might have been the Archangel Michael come down from Heaven to save them.

"It is all over," the Duke said, "but I am afraid you will have to ride home. There is no way we can get a carriage up here."

They went outside as he spoke.

Kasia saw two grooms leading two horses which she knew were intended for Simon and herself.

The Duke's horse was led by a young man whom she saw was armed.

Walking away from them were the four kidnappers escorted by five of the Duke's men.

It was light enough for Kasia to recognise that Bates was one of them.

The four other men she guessed had been with the Duke in the Army.

Without being told, she was certain he had picked the men who were good shots.

They would also carry out his orders to the letter.

The kidnappers had therefore surrendered rather than be killed.

She was aware that Bill with his wounded arm was being assisted across the field.

The Duke did not say anything.

He merely lifted Simon onto one of the horses, then turned towards Kasia.

She looked up at him and knew that he was thinking of how he had kissed her.

She wanted, as she had never wanted anything in her whole life, for him to kiss her again.

Just for a moment they looked at each other.

Then the Duke lifted her onto the saddle.

As he did so there was a sudden tumbling noise which made him look over his shoulder.

Sharply, in the voice of an Officer giving orders, he said:

"Quick! Quick! Move away! Hurry!"

As he spoke he took hold of the reins of Kasia's horse and started to run into the open field.

After a moment's pause Simon followed, so did the grooms and the one leading the Duke's stallion.

The Duke stopped about thirty yards from the Watch-Tower.

He drew Kasia's horse to a standstill.

She looked back and realised that the noise which had startled him had grown louder.

She saw that the Watch-Tower was leaning over sideways.

She drew in her breath.

Then suddenly with a tremendous crash the whole top of the building in which she and Simon had been imprisoned, fell to the ground.

A cloud of dust rose and as it subsided they would see that only half of the Watch-Tower remained.

It was then Kasia was aware that she was holding tightly to the Duke's hand.

In an inarticulate voice she managed to say:

"That . . that was . . where you . . climbed up! It . . it could have . . killed . . you!"

"And you too, my precious," the Duke answered.

Hearing the endearment, her eyes turned from the Watch-Tower to him.

145

She felt as if he took her in his arms and the world seemed to stand still.

Then he said abruptly, as if it was an effort to speak:

"Now we can go home in peace."

He walked towards his stallion and mounted it.

"Join the others, John," he said to the groom. "We do not want any of those rogues escaping at the last minute."

"Oi'll make sure o' that, Yer Grace!" John said.

He rode off quickly to where the other men had stopped a little distance from them.

They were staring at the fallen Watch-Tower as if they could not believe their eyes.

As John joined them they turned round.

Apparently on the orders of those guarding them, they started to walk slowly over the rough ground.

Bill was still groaning and clutching his injured arm.

The Duke moved ahead and Simon, who was beside Kasia, said excitedly:

"I have never ridden at night before. It was very, very clever of you, Uncle Darcy, to come and rescue us. Miss Watson and I were trying to tell you where we were."

"The Power of Thought!" Kasia said quickly so that the Duke would understand.

"I read your code," he replied.

"I prayed you would understand."

"I did," he said briefly, "and it was what I expected from you."

There was a depth in his voice that made her blush.

146

Suddenly, as if after all he was in a hurry to get back to the Castle, the Duke spurred his horse and rode a little faster.

When they reached the stables, it was to find that not only the grooms, but almost everyone in the Castle, who had been left behind was there.

As they appeared a little cheer went up.

It was so sincere that Kasia felt the tears come into her eyes.

Someone lifted Simon off his horse.

He saw Nanny, ran to her, and she put her arms around him.

Kasia could hear him telling her excitedly what had happened.

She was then aware that the Duke was standing beside her, waiting to lift her from the saddle.

"I have brought you home," he said so that only she could hear.

"You were . . wonderful!" she whispered.

When they went into the Castle there was food waiting for them in the Dining-Room.

Simon announced that he was very hungry.

"I will join you in a few minutes," Kasia said to the Duke.

She thought as she ran up the stairs that she could not bear him to see her looking so dishevelled and dirty.

The wagon had been none too clean.

The floor on which she and Simon had been obliged to sit was thick with dust.

She washed and one of the housemaids helped her to put on a fresh gown.

It took her less than ten minutes and she had no wish to linger because she wanted to be with the Duke.

When she joined them in the Dining-Room, Simon already had a bowl of soup in front of him.

"I insist first that you have a glass of champagne," the Duke said as she appeared. "You have not only been through a very frightening experience but we are also celebrating your return to civilisation."

"It was frightening," Kasia agreed, "but Simon was very brave. You can be proud of him."

"I am," the Duke replied.

"If I had had a gun," Simon said, "I would have shot them like you shot that horrid man called Bill."

"He will be in pain with that arm for some time," the Duke said, "and he will have a long prison sentence to go with it!"

"I am glad they are going to prison," Simon said. "They are very wicked men!"

"I think what frightened me more than anything else was knowing that you were in the Watch-Tower," the Duke said. "I had been told over and over again that it was unsafe and might collapse at any moment."

"And yet . . you climbed up . . it!" Kasia said softly.

"To be with you," the Duke replied. "It was no worse than climbing mountains in Portugal or the Pyrenees."

Kasia guessed that these were two of the places where he had won medals for gallantry.

"If I had a medal, I would give it to you!" she said.

"We will talk about that later," the Duke replied, and his eyes were on her lips.

It seemed to Kasia as if she was moving in a dream.

She had no idea what she ate or drank.

Nanny came to collect Simon and he got up from the table and put his arms around Kasia saying:

"I was brave, was I not, and I did try to protect you."

"You were wonderful!" Kasia said.

"Next time I will shoot those wicked men with my gun!" he said firmly.

He moved to the Duke and to his surprise hugged him.

"Nanny says you are a dare-devil, Uncle Darcy. I am going to be just like you and you must teach me how to shoot."

"I will do that," the Duke said, "but of course you realise that if you are going to be like me you will have to read."

He paused a moment and then went on:

"Otherwise I could not have read Miss Watson's letter, and I would never have known where you were."

Simon thought this over for a moment. Then he said:

"All right. I will read, if I can shoot."

"That is a deal!" the Duke replied.

Simon hugged him again, then ran off with Nanny.

He was talking about what wicked men he would shoot when he had bullets in his gun.

The Duke looked at Kasia with a smile.

She was thinking he would be as clever with his own children when he had them.

Without speaking, they went into the Drawing-Room.

He stood looking at her and she wondered what he was about to say.

Their eyes met, he moved towards her and she was in his arms.

As she waited, her lips raised to his, he said:

"How can you be so lovely, so incredibly beautiful, that it is impossible to live without you?"

Then he was kissing her, not gently, but wildly, fiercely, passionately, as if he defied Fate to take her from him.

To Kasia, it was as if Heaven's doors had opened and she had flown inside.

She was no longer human, but one with the angels.

The Duke's kisses made her feel as if the moonlight was shining through her.

At the same time, she was his and they were no longer two people, but one.

She knew then it was how she had felt since the first day she had met him.

Although she had not understood it, her heart had spoken to his heart and her soul to his soul.

"I love you!" the Duke was saying. "God, how I love you!"

Then he was kissing her again.

Only when Kasia thought it was impossible to feel such ecstasy and not die from the wonder of it, did the Duke ask:

"How soon will you marry me? I cannot wait and I am desperately afraid that someone might take you from me."

"I . . I love . . you," Kasia answered.

"Then that is all that matters," the Duke said.

He kissed her until they were both breathless, then he drew her down onto the sofa.

"We must make plans, my darling," he said. "I could not face again what I faced today, when I thought those devils might have hurt you, or that I might not be able to find you."

Kasia gave a little sigh.

"You mean . . when they had the money . . they might have . . left us . . to starve?"

"They might have done anything!" the Duke said hastily. "That is why I want you with me every day and every – night."

There was a little pause before he said the last word.

Then he added:

"I have lain awake wanting you until I thought I would go mad!"

"I thought and prayed for you," Kasia said, "and what was so wonderful was that you understood where we were. Simon and I both prayed that you would understand my code."

"I thought you were telling me where to look," the Duke said simply, "and just as I have been able to read your thoughts, I was able to read what you were trying to convey to me."

"I think . . that is what . . Love means," Kasia murmured.

"You have not answered my question," the Duke said. "When will you marry me?"

"Are you really asking me to be your wife, not knowing who I am?"

"You were very positive you would not tell me," the Duke said with a smile, "but now, as your future husband, I feel I am entitled to be let into the secret."

Kasia felt he was feeling for words.

Then he said:

"I have just thought of something – when you wrote your name at the bottom of the note, I presume from dictation – I seemed to have heard of the name 'Kasia' before. Now I remember where!"

He got up as he spoke and went to the stool in front of the fireplace.

Kasia was aware that, just as her Father had them, the newspapers were laid out on it.

The Duke picked up the *Morning Post*.

He brought it to her, pointing out an item in the 'Wanted' column.

Kasia took it from him and following the direction of his finger, she read:

"Kasia, forgive me, and come home.
I miss you!

R.R."

She read the message, then gave a little cry.

"I have won! I have won!"

"You have won – what?" the Duke enquired.

"The battle with my Father," she answered.

"It was from him you ran away?"

Kasia nodded.

He gave a deep sigh.

"If you knew the agony I have been through imagining that it was from a husband, or a lover."

Kasia looked at him in astonishment.

"H.how could you . . think such . . a thing?"

"I love you and I want you, and I promise you I shall be a very jealous husband."

"There will be no need for you to be jealous of anyone!" she said softly.

"I thought today that I was the first person who had ever kissed you," the Duke said. "Is that so?"

"Of course it is! No one has kissed me . . except you."

The Duke would have pulled her against him, but she said:

"Let me tell you why I ran away."

"Why did you?"

"Because my Father, whose house is on the other side of Berkeley Square from yours, told me I was to marry an elderly Peer called Lord Stefelton!"

"Marry him? Why should your Father have wanted that?"

Kasia hesitated for a moment. Then she said:

"Papa is very rich . . and he is so . . afraid I will marry a fortune-hunter."

The Duke laughed.

"So that is why you ran away! My darling, I may be many things, but I am not a fortune-hunter!"

"I know that," Kasia said, "and I was determined I would not marry any man I did not love. Papa said it was utterly impossible for me to earn a penny piece for myself!"

"Well, now you can tell him he is wrong," the Duke said. "You have earned a week's wages, not once, but a thousand times, and I will pay you in any coinage you like."

"I would . . prefer it in . . kisses," Kasia said, "and you do . . understand that if you will . . marry me, I shall . . marry the man . . I love."

"I am going to marry you as quickly as possible. Apart from anything else, there is a great deal to do here, and you know that, like me, Simon cannot do without you."

"I love Simon, I love the Castle, and I love you!" Kasia cried.

The Duke knew there was a little note of passion in her voice he had never heard before.

It brought the fire into his eyes.

Then he was kissing her with long possessive, passionate kisses.

They changed the moonlight that was still within Kasia into little flames of fire.

She did not understand what it meant.

She only knew that once again the Heavens opened.

The Duke was carrying her into a world of such beauty, light and love, that she knew what they had found together was what had always been in their hearts.

"I love . . you! I love . . you!" she murmured.

Then as the Duke drew her closer still, she knew that the wonder and glory of it was there for all Eternity.

Other books by Barbara Cartland

Romantic Novels, over 500, the most recently published being:

Seek the Stars
Running Away to Love
Look with the Heart
Safe in Paradise
Love in the Ruins
A Coronation of Love
A Duel of Jewels
The Duke is Trapped
Just a Wonderful Dream
Love and Cheetah

Drena and the Duke
A Dog, a Horse and a Heart
Never Lose Love
Spirit of Love
The Eyes of Love
The Duke's Dilemma
Saved by a Saint
Beyond the Stars
The Innocent Imposter
The Incomparable

The Dream and the Glory (In aid of the St. John Ambulance Brigade)

Autobiographical and Biographical:

The Isthmus Years 1919–1939
The Years of Opportunity 1939–1945
I Search for Rainbows 1945–1976
We Danced All Night 1919–1929
Ronald Cartland (With a foreword by Sir Winston Churchill)
Polly – My Wonderful Mother
I Seek the Miraculous

Historical:

Bewitching Women
The Outrageous Queen (The Story of Queen Christina of Sweden)
The Scandalous Life of King Carol
The Private Life of Charles II
The Private Life of Elizabeth, Empress of Austria
Josephine, Empress of France
Diane de Poitiers
Metternich – The Passionate Diplomat
A Year of Royal Days
Royal Jewels
Royal Eccentrics
Royal Lovers

Sociology:

You in the Home	Etiquette
The Fascinating Forties	The Many Facets of Love
Marriage for Moderns	Sex and the Teenager
Be Vivid, Be Vital	The Book of Charm
Love, Life and Sex	Living Together
Vitamins for Vitality	The Youth Secret
Husbands and Wives	The Magic of Honey
Men are Wonderful	The Book of Beauty and Health

Keep Young and Beautiful by Barbara Cartland and Elinor Glyn
Etiquette for Love and Romance
Barbara Cartland's Book of Health

General:

Barbara Cartland's Book of Useless Information with a Foreword by the
    Earl Mountbatten of Burma.
    (In aid of the United World Colleges)
Love and Lovers (Picture Book)
The Light of Love (Prayer Book)
Barbara Cartland's Scrapbook
(In aid of the Royal Photographic Museum)
Romantic Royal Marriages
Barbara Cartland's Book of Celebrities
Getting Older, Growing Younger

Verse:

Lines on Life and Love

Music:

An Album of Love Songs
sung with the Royal Philharmonic Orchestra

Films:

A Hazard of Hearts
The Lady and the Highwayman
A Ghost in Monte Carlo
A Duel of Hearts

Cartoons:

Barbara Cartland Romances (Book of Cartoons)
has recently been published in the U.S.A., Great Britain,
and other parts of the world.

Children:

A Children's Pop-Up Book: "Princess to the Rescue"

Videos:

A Hazard of Hearts
The Lady and the Highwayman
A Ghost in Monte Carlo
A Duel of Hearts

Cookery:

Barbara Cartland's Health Food Cookery Book
Food for Love
Magic of Honey Cookbook
Recipes for Lovers
The Romance of Food

Editor of:

"The Common Problem" by Ronald Cartland (with a preface by the Rt. Hon. the Earl of Selborne, P.C.)
Barbara Cartland's Library of Love
Library of Ancient Wisdom
"Written with Love" Passionate love letters selected by Barbara Cartland

Drama:

Blood Money
French Dressing

Philosophy:

Touch the Stars

Radio Operetta:

The Rose and the Violet
(Music by Mark Lubbock) Performed in 1942

Radio Plays:

The Caged Bird: An episode in the life of Elizabeth Empress of Austria Performed in 1957